BROTHER MOOSE

Brother Moose

by
Betty Levin

 Greenwillow Books
New York

Printed in the United States of America   First Edition   10 9 8 7 6 5 4 3 2 1

Library of Congress Cataloging-in-Publication Data
Levin, Betty.
Brother moose/by Betty Levin.
p.   cm.
Summary: In the late 1800s, two orphan girls, aided by an Indian and his grandson, make a perilous trip to Maine to find a family.
ISBN 0-688-09266-7
[1. Orphans—Fiction.   2. Frontier and pioneer life—Fiction.
3. Indians of North America—Fiction.]   I. Title.
PZ7.L5759Br 1990   [Fic]—dc20   89-34437   CIP   AC

For Ethel and Paul
and
Jill and John

Contents

BROTHER MOOSE

1/Parting

Nell could feel the conductor's fingers pinch through all her layers of clothing. She tried to twist around, to make sure Louisa was close behind, but those bony fingers tightened on her shoulder and propelled her forward. How was he to know that Louisa was the one who needed guiding?

When he stopped and yanked Nell onto the wooden seat, he turned to reach for Louisa. Only she shrank from him and shot a wild glance toward the door.

"Over here," Nell called. It was hard to sound calm and cheerful when she was terrified that Louisa would bolt from the train. "You can sit by the window. Louisa, here."

The conductor shrugged. No doubt he made the usual mistake of assuming Louisa was older because she was so much bigger than Nell. As soon as the girls were settled, he went off to attend to other passengers.

"Are we still in Canada?" Louisa whispered.

Nell nodded.

"Why did Miss Kingston leave us?"

"She has to go back to Nova Scotia, to where we came from. We're in a different province now. We're in New Brunswick. We're almost there."

"Almost where?"

Nell didn't want to mention their new homes. Both girls dreaded the coming separation. "Where we're going," Nell answered, and was unable to think of anything reassuring to add.

The conductor ushered a lady to the seat across the aisle. Nodding toward Nell and Louisa, he informed the lady that they were Home children on their way to their new situations. Nell offered the lady an uncertain smile. Louisa scowled and drew spirals in the dust on the window glass.

"Are you sisters?" the lady inquired.

"No, ma'am. Well, almost. We've been together." For Louisa's sake, Nell went on. "We'll still be close by, Louisa and me."

Suddenly, fiercely, Louisa flattened her hand and smeared out all the spirals on the window.

The woman drew in her skirt to let three cigar-smoking men pass. One of them kicked a spittoon into the aisle. Nell caught a glimpse of a brown trickle down the side of it. She turned toward the window.

The steam whistle hooted. The train lurched. Thrust forward, Louisa hunched down. Nell watched her anxiously. She had the look she sometimes got when she was about to rock and moan. But she had promised not to. It was important for her new family to know the best of her before she showed them her worst.

As the train chugged away from the depot, steam billowed up around the window. They went swaying and listing through a dank, moiling cloud. Nell could see her own face in the glass. Her heart sank. Her straight brown hair was pulled so tight, the skin seemed drawn back with it. Was it the grime and smoke on the glass that made her look so wan? "Do try to look sunny and robust," Miss Kingston had instructed with a sigh, as if she knew she asked for the impossible. Nell rubbed her cheeks. Only now the smoke was thinning, and with it Nell's image. Nell gazed at gray buildings, stagnant water, a tangle of weeds turned yellow and red by the frost.

How far had they to go? Nell had no idea. If Miss Kingston had told her, Nell had no recollection of it. After the first train from Nova Scotia, Miss Kingston had recited a list of dos and don'ts while they waited to board the stagecoach. It had been hard to pay close attention with so much to see all around them. The stage itself had been thrilling to behold, shiny red decorations painted over the yellow body and with red wheels to match. But the ride had shaken every bone loose, and every thought from Nell's mind. With dust in her mouth and grit in her eyes, very little remained of Miss Kingston's instructions.

Except for the packet. Nell remembered that Miss Kingston had cautioned Nell to save it until it was truly needed. Leaning down, Nell groped beneath the seat. There was the satchel she, herself, had made from a worn-out coverlet. Inside were a second skirt and blouse, a shift and flannel petticoat, a nightdress and stockings. Also her special possessions, the hairbrush and the merino shawl. And, yes, here was the packet Miss Kingston had shoved in on top of everything else.

"By and by, we'll have something to eat," Nell told Louisa. "A picnic."

"I'm thirsty," Louisa whispered.

Nell was thirsty, too. "There may be a stop with water." Only what if they had to pay for a drink? They had no money. "Or maybe we'll get there so soon, we won't need to stop."

Swaying, the train rumbled over a high, narrow bridge. Far below them, a river snaked around a settlement. The houses looked like toys, the log boom where the river curved back on itself like some game played with matchsticks.

Louisa covered her eyes.

"We won't fall," Nell said to her. "The bridge is used to the train coming over it."

But Louisa couldn't look until the train had regained solid ground. When it slowed and chugged into a small depot, Nell's heart began to pound. This might be the stop where Louisa had to get off all by herself.

The conductor appeared carrying a case and a box. A couple followed him down the aisle past the children and the lady and past the men with cigars.

"It's all right," Nell murmured. "We're all right." It wasn't this town, this stop, for Louisa.

"I'm still thirsty," Louisa whispered.

he lady across from them bought apples through her window
m a vendor. After the train started forward again and picked up
speed, she handed two of the apples across to Nell. Nell thanked
her for Louisa, as well as for herself. The apples were crisp and
juicy. Other passengers opened baskets with food and bottles of
cider and water. Nell told Louisa that apples were the best way to
quench your thirst. She didn't touch the packet in her satchel. She
knew that bread would only make them thirsty again.

The train passed through a dreary landscape of burned forest,
with only occasional farms to relieve the lifelessness. The train
stopped again at a little house beside the track with a road winding up toward a small cluster of buildings. The lady stood up,
smiled at Nell, and left. The conductor dragged her bag out for
her and handed it down the steps. Then he lit a fire in the stove at
the end of the car.

Soon the warmth would reach the girls. Nell missed her coat. It
had been mended and passed on to one of the smaller girls in the
Home. Miss Kingston believed the merino shawl would be ade-
quate through the autumn.

"You must remember to tell Mrs. Warburton about your
gloves," Nell reminded Louisa. The gloves had been lost at a
stagecoach stop. "Don't wait till your fingers get blue."

Louisa nodded. She didn't speak.

After a while the car filled with wood smoke. The voices around
Nell and Louisa slurred and thickened. Faces turned from the low
sun; heads nodded.

Nell woke suddenly as the train shuddered to a halt beside a
nondescript building with wagons and people waiting beside it. It
was hard for Nell to rouse herself, but here was the conductor,
beckoning. Nell had to wake Louisa. She brushed back the fair
curls that stuck to Louisa's flushed cheek.

"We're here," Nell told her. She grabbed Louisa's bag and
started to lead her to the door, but the conductor nodded Nell
back. "She needs me," Nell tried to explain.

"Only the big girl," the conductor said to her. "Just the one." He took Louisa firmly by the arm, propelled her around in front of him, and set her down the steps.

Nell stood immobilized. How could it happen so fast, without a word of parting?

"Over here," said one of the men by the spittoon. "You can see from this window."

Instead, Nell dove onto the lady's empty seat. She caught a glimpse of a woman surrounded by children. Was that Mrs. Warburton? Was one of the children Louisa? The engine hissed and chugged forward. Nell craned but couldn't locate Louisa. She saw WOODVILLE painted on the end of the wooden building, a depot, after all. The train pulled around a mill, and the depot vanished. Nell returned to her seat.

She took up her satchel and placed it beside the window. Now Louisa's seat didn't look so empty. Nell would be getting off soon, anyway. The Home had made a special point of placing the girls close together.

When the train slowed again, Nell straightened her jacket and gathered up the satchel. There was a squeal. A tremendous jolt nearly knocked her from the seat.

Passengers leaned out windows. Voices rose. One man strode to the end of the car, spoke to the brakeman, and called back to his companions that the tracks had to be cleared. Most of the passengers took advantage of the delay to step out into the twilight. Nell wanted to go, too, but she was afraid of being left behind.

When the conductor called the passengers in, Nell heard them talking about a calf carcass that had blocked the train. One man said it looked like a bear kill, but most of them wagered it was Indian mischief. The Indians hereabouts resented the railroad coming through their hunting grounds; they settled old grudges this way.

"What are we waiting for now?" someone demanded.

"Tracks have to be sanded," the conductor told them. "Then we'll be on our way."

"Yes, and soon past dark" came a complaint.

Nell gazed out at charred tree stumps and blackened trunks. She could see nothing beyond this grim wasteland. Even the pond they passed looked dead, with tree skeletons standing gaunt at its edge.

The train slowed again without jolting anyone. As soon as it halted, some of the passengers rose at once, but the conductor stopped them. The train was just letting off a passenger, that was all. He nodded at Nell.

Her heart skipped a beat.

One of the men with cigars looked out the window. He said, "Someone meeting her?"

The conductor told him it was all arranged. Maybe whoever it was had gone off to attend to something else when the train didn't show up on time. Anyway, the girl was expected.

Nell stood clutching her satchel. Suddenly this dirty, smoky railway car felt familiar and safe. "Isn't there a depot?" she asked.

"Just the bridge," the conductor informed her. "It's the only bridge over Musquash Stream." He lifted her down and set the satchel beside her. "There'll be someone along, have no fear." He swung onto the car platform and waved to the brakeman, who shouted to the engineer.

Nell watched the train mount the wooden bridge. The planks rumbled under the tracks. Then the train disappeared in a mass of black smoke with sparks flying up in a shower from the huge stack. Out of the darkening sky, ash fell about her like gray petals dissolving into indistinct smudges on her hair and sleeves.

Where was the road? If only she knew what direction to look in. By now Louisa must be home. There would be lamplight and new faces.

Nell pulled her shawl from the satchel. It felt good around her shoulders, somehow safer. Besides, the evening air had a bite.

She walked onto the bridge. But standing between the tracks gave her an icy feeling, so she went back to the satchel and sat on a log. She pulled out the packet Miss Kingston had left with her and unwrapped it with care. Just as she thought: bread. She broke it in half and ate what she held. After that she had to eat the rest of it, too. And now she had nothing. It didn't matter, though. Soon Mr. and Mrs. Fowler would come for her. Soon she, too, would be inside a house with a plate of supper set before her in the lamplight.

2/Robbers!

In the last of the light the dead trees took on a moss gray sheen. Nell pulled the shawl over her head and knotted it under her chin. The next time she looked around, the trees had gone black.

Could the train conductor have been mistaken? What if the Fowlers were waiting for her at a bridge over another stream? Still, Nell told herself, she could always follow the tracks back to Woodville. She wondered how long that would take.

Something she couldn't see whirred overhead. Nell cringed. All in an instant a dark shape swept the tracks. Nell felt the rush of it and heard a thin, piercing cry that left in its wake a listening silence. Nell opened her mouth, then shut it again. *Think of a song.* She tried to sing—"'Oh, Susannah, oh don't you cry for me'"— but she couldn't remember the rest of the words. What about "Give to the Wind Thy Fears?" "'Hope and be undismayed,'" she sang in a quavering voice. "'God hears thy sighs and counts thy tears—'" Tears. How could she keep from crying? She cleared her throat, and then she heard branches breaking, hooves stomping, and the unmistakable squeal and rattle of an approaching wagon.

Standing straight, her satchel in both hands, Nell peered into the gloom. "Mr. Fowler?" she called. "It's me, Nell Haskins. I'm here."

The horse pulled the wagon into the clearing. She stared up at the man on the seat. He was hard to see in the dark, hard to find under a robe draped over his shoulders and his deep, wide-brimmed hat.

"Get in," he ordered. "Waited long enough."

She walked around the huge horse and tried to hand her satchel to the man. He grabbed her wrist and hauled her up beside him, satchel and all.

"Thank you, Mr. Fowler," she said. "I'm sorry I was late. It was something on the tracks that stopped the train."

"Mr. Fowler's gone. Fixed you coming before Berry Ripe Moon." The man turned the horse away from the bridge. Nell could hardly see ahead, but the horse seemed to know how to pick its way through the trees.

"I had to stay at the Home until they found a place for my . . . almost sister. Where did Mr. Fowler go to?"

"Winter work," said the man. "Logging."

Nell wondered whether the Home had any idea that she was too late for what the Fowlers wanted.

"You go to her, Mrs. Fowler, she wait long time."

Nell gripped the seat as the wagon jounced over something. Feeling suddenly relieved and tired, she shivered. "I've been a long time, too," she said. "My almost-sister stopped in Woodville. Do you know about Louisa?"

The man turned toward Nell. She could just barely make out his eyes beneath the black brim. They were dark and registered nothing.

"I been to Woodville already." He gestured back over his shoulder. "Took corn to mill, load up with meal and flour. For her, Jessie, understand, not for me, Joe."

Nell couldn't tell from the way he spoke whether he was a hired man or a member of the Fowler family. "Are you Joe?" she asked.

Nodding, he thumped his chest with his left hand. Only there was something wrong with it. The hand looked white and knobby. It wasn't all there. Nell couldn't stifle a cry. She shrank back so fast, she swung sideways. It was important to hold on, but to what?

Joe caught her as she fell, yanked her onto the seat, then let go so that he could grab her dangling shawl.

"Better in back," he told her. "Under rubber blanket. Room

there." As she stumbled onto the load, he handed over her satchel and his own robe. Groping for the edge of the rubber cover, she crawled and huddled until at last she landed in a kind of nest between the flour sacks. She pressed the satchel to her face to ward off the dust and the rankness of the robe, a furry hide of some kind. "Buffalo robe warm," Joe declared from above. "You see."

Of course she couldn't see. She heard him slap the reins and cluck to the horse. The wagon rumbled forward. She gave herself to the lumbering rhythm, to the absolute darkness.

It seemed to her that she had only been asleep a moment when everything jolted, someone yelled. In a fit of panic she tried to throw off the robe and the rubber blanket. She couldn't find her way out from under them. She would have to wait for Joe to help her. Any minute now he would lift the covers and she would sit up and gulp the frosty night air.

Waiting, she listened to the tumult of voices, the loudest one grating and booming with harsh laughter. Most of what they said was impossible to understand, but not the thuds and grunts. Someone was being beaten. Nell went very still inside. Things were tossed onto the wagon. It creaked and groaned. Did she hear human groans as well? She curled into a tight ball. The wagon started forward. Nell strained to catch the accent of the man who called himself Joe, but she couldn't hear his voice among the others.

The horse kept slowing to a walk. The reins slapped, forcing him to a trot, but it didn't last. Fast, slow, fast, slow. The bumping and swaying made Nell's ears hum.

She came awake when the wagon stopped again and the voices rose in argument. One said they needed to get more distance on them. Another warned that if the horse went down, they'd lose him and the wagon, too. A branch snapped, the wagon jiggled, and then there was a whoosh and a crack. The wagon lurched.

Nell longed to call Joe's name, but she knew better than to utter a sound. Something terrible had happened. The voices she heard were those of robbers. They had seized the wagon as pirates seize ships. Was Joe lying helpless in the woods?

Nell resisted the lulling motion, hooves plodding, harness creaking, and the rattling wheels. The men weren't talking much anymore. She guessed they were sleepy.

The horse kept slowing until he halted. The men spoke of camping until daylight. "But leave him hitched up," the grating voice ordered. "We might need to get going sudden."

Soon there was another crackling sound. Nell's fingers crept and fumbled until she was able to raise the edge of the rubber blanket. She smelled wood burning. "Ain't doing much, this dinky fire," one man grumbled. Another's answer was lost to her as the horse tossed his head, the rein rings and bit clanking. "Tie the horse?" said one. "What?" came the reply, and then, "Guess so."

It was hard to wait for these men to go to sleep. At the first snores she wanted to climb down and run away. If only she had some idea of where to look for Joe. As she peeled back the covers, the wagon suddenly creaked. She froze. But it was just because the horse was leaning down to rub his muzzle against his foreleg. Nell rose to her knees. There were three men lying around what remained of the fire. She tried to peer at the faces, but one was turned away, one covered by a hand, the last by a jacket. They had stolen the Fowlers' horse and wagon. Were they murderers as well?

She was too high up to jump to the ground. She had to climb around onto the seat, which took her farther from the robbers and closer to the horse between the shafts. Poor horse, she thought. If only she knew how to release him.

And then it occurred to her that she might be able to drive him away. She glanced back at the men, lumps with lumps that must be packs strewn on the ground. She looked along the broad expanse of the horse to his drooping head. Reaching for the reins looped over the whip socket, she pulled as quietly as she could. It took a while for the horse to feel the tug, to raise his head. When she pulled on just one rein and turned him, she could tell that he wasn't tethered.

She looked all around. The trees on her right would block the wagon. She had to keep tugging on the left rein. Now what? She tried clucking to him but was afraid of waking the robbers. She pulled a long, tapered stick from the whip socket. Thinking again, poor horse, she stood tall and swung it down on him with all her might.

As he lunged forward he turned so sharply, she was flung to her knees. She whacked him once more and then had to use both hands to cling to the footboard. She felt sure the wagon sounded louder than a railway engine at full steam. Surely the men would hear it and catch her. The horse was plunging at an awkward gallop. She couldn't figure out what was wrong with him, couldn't find the reins, couldn't regain the seat.

She thought she heard shouts, but she didn't dare look back. All she could do was hang on for dear life while the horse dragged the wagon over logs and rocks, until somehow he brought it onto the road. Now she could see that the reins were caught under one foreleg and around the shaft. Yet the horse kept on. Everything slapped and banged so hard, she thought any moment the wagon would break apart. When they came to a fork in the road, the horse never faltered, striking out to the left and pounding clumsily, his harness lathered with sweat.

He only slowed when the road forded a shallow stream. Hearing his tearing breath, Nell was caught between pity and fear. She had to let him stop. Then she slid her way down to stand beside him. Could she get him to pick up his foot? He was the biggest horse she had ever seen. Leaning against his sweat-soaked leg, she stooped over to grab his shaggy fetlock. She might as well try to get an oak to part from its roots. The horse lowered his head as far as the rein allowed, his mouth wide, his nostrils flared and wet. She could see all his enormous, yellowed teeth.

Kneeling at the stream, she raised her cupped hands to him. He slobbered the water out of them. She tried again. This time he sucked; in one second all the water she could carry was gone.

It would take hours this way, and even though she must have left the robbers far behind, they still might come looking for the wagon and the horse. She went back to his foot and slapped it; he didn't budge. Then she saw the buckle on the reins. All she had to do was reach and unbuckle it to untangle the part around his leg. Hitching up her skirt, she climbed onto the shaft. After a struggle she had two rein ends. One she looped around the whip socket; the other she let drop to the ground, and then she pulled it free.

After that she let the horse drink on his own. He gulped first, then sloshed his brown muzzle in the water. She clambered back onto the seat, buckled the reins again, and stepped on them while she picked up the stick. She tried to hit him gently. He swished his tail. When she hit him harder, his head came up from the water. She knew too much was bad for a hot horse, so she hauled in the reins as hard as she could. For a moment she thought he was going to fight her. Then he lumbered on, pulling the wagon across the stream and over the rutted road.

As soon as he set a good walking pace, she gave him his head. They were coming into meadowland now. Mist swirled up from boggy places and cleared the hillocks that rose gently all around. Up ahead, there was a kind of island of trees well off the road that might protect them while they rested. Nell had to flog the horse over a ditch. He strained and drew the wagon, which bumped and nearly caught in the roots and rubble. He wanted to graze the long, thin grass, but she made him press on, to get them partway around the tree island.

Her hands had red welts from the leather. She rubbed them on her skirt until the tingling stopped. The horse was crunching small green apples. Nell climbed down to gather some, too. The juice squirted—tart, almost bitter—but she was too hungry to mind. The horse roamed about gorging on apples until Nell grew worried for him and had to resort to the stick again to drag him back from the trees. "I'm sorry," she told him, meeting his reproachful eye. "It's to keep you from the colic." He snorted, found grass, and began to yank up great tufts of it instead.

Nell climbed onto the wagon, emptied her skirtful of apples into her satchel, and, with the reins wrapped around her, lay on her side in the morning sunshine. Somewhere nearby, wasps droned around the fruit rotting on the ground and hummed her to sleep.

3/Which Way?

In adventure stories you were supposed to let the sun help you find your way. But Nell didn't know how to use the sun. Even if she could tell east from west, she had no idea which direction led to the Fowler farm.

But the horse ought to know. Horses and dogs were supposed to head for home. When she clucked to him, he twitched one ear. She didn't have the heart to whip him again. She could see the dark streaks where the harness shifted, ugly sweat marks on his brown coat. She yanked the reins and slapped their loose ends against the footboard. That worked. With an answering snort, he ambled toward the road. She held the reins loosely so that he could lean and stretch as he pulled the wagon over the ditch. And then he would be able to choose which way to go.

Only he didn't turn; he just went straight across. That left the wagon straddling the road.

"No," she commanded, "go home." She raised the reins to make him back onto the road. She could hear another wagon approaching.

"Hey," a man called to her. "You're blocking the way."

"I'm trying," Nell answered.

Without another word, the man jumped down from his wagon, strode around to Nell's horse, grabbed the cheek straps in both hands, and backed the horse onto the road. "Which way?" he asked.

"I'm looking for Mr. and Mrs. Fowler. Do you know them? This is their horse and wagon."

"Don't know any Fowlers," he said. "You're all alone?" His hand traveled along the horse's neck and down the shoulder to the foreleg. "Nice animal," he declared, glancing back at his own bony team. He walked the length of the Fowler wagon. Nell swiveled, watching uneasily. At the rear he yanked up a corner of the rubber blanket and jabbed underneath. Nell wanted him to leave the wagon alone. While she was trying to thank him for helping her with the horse, the man lifted a full sack and shouldered it.

"What are you doing?" she asked him.

He turned a gap-toothed grin on her. "Lightening your load, little lady."

"No," she protested. "Don't."

"See, I've a team to do the hauling. You've just got the one horse."

"No, leave me alone!" she shouted at him.

"Tell you what," he said. "I can just hitch your horse to my wagon. Then you won't have to worry about a thing."

Nell screamed and slapped the reins. The horse swerved and took off, forcing the man to dive out of the way. Saplings snapped as the two right wheels rode the edge of the ditch. "Come on!" she yelled at the horse. She had to get the wagon past the man's. One sapling sprang back just as the man lunged out to stop her, and smacked him head-on. The horse broke into a gallop.

She kept him going until she reached a crossroad with a few log houses around it. Nell's heart quickened. There were barns and small fields between the houses and the woods beyond. Children were chasing each other around a well. Calling to them, she asked the name of this place.

"Medet," a little one answered.

"Medet Settlement," another corrected.

Medet had a familiar ring to it. Nell was sure Miss Kingston had mentioned it to her.

"Which house does Mrs. Fowler live in?" she asked.

The children stared at her, looked at each other, then shook their heads. There wasn't any Mrs. Fowler here.

Nell blinked back tears and clucked to the horse. On they went, straight on. Later, when she heard the distant hoot of a steam whistle, she began to think about finding her way back to Woodville. Someone at the flour mill should be able to direct her to the Fowler farm. The mournful whistle died away. She wondered where the train was going.

Darkness closed in rapidly. Nell kept imagining that she smelled fresh bread. Her stomach clenched with hunger, and she gazed longingly at a solitary cabin set back amid tree stumps in a small clearing. A dog barked, and for just one moment a hand drew back a curtain, showing a square of warm, yellow light.

The next farm she came to had a harvested cornfield farther along. The horse yearned toward it, as if he could tell it harbored overlooked ears of corn among the stubble. She loosened the reins and allowed him to pick his way up an embankment and into the cornfield. A dog barked here, too, but didn't appear. Nell guessed it was tied for the night. She hoped no one else heard the wagon clattering over the soft ground.

Suddenly the horse stopped and nosed down. Nell could hear him crunch; she smelled the milky juice of the corn. Nell clambered down and groped through rustling stalks at the edge of the field. Here, where the trees must shade the outer rows and the scythe had passed them by, she found tiny ears, barely formed. She ate them the way the horse did, cobs and all.

She supposed she was stealing, breaking the law and God's commandment both. She had only been on her own a little while, and already she was stooping to the lowest life. "But really," she whispered to the horse, "we're only stealing from the birds and the rabbits."

He went on chomping for all he was worth. She thought it must be easier to be an animal who didn't have to worry about right and wrong. Then she recalled the beatings and his thirst and the sweaty harness. And what about those listless, scrawny horses driven by that man who stole the flour?

Already on her knees, Nell said her prayers just as she had at bedtime in the Home. Louisa might be murmuring the same words at this very moment, only in her special way, like someone who has memorized a foreign language without comprehending it.

After Nell prayed for Louisa and for Joe, she decided not to spend the night in this field. The farmer might rise early, and he might not agree with her that she had only stolen from the small wild creatures of the woods and grasslands.

She let the horse browse on weeds along the roadside. When he stopped to sleep, she tried to stay awake, just in case that man came looking for them. Common sense told her he was home in bed somewhere, but common sense didn't quell her fear.

In the morning the horse plodded on, veering now and then to snatch another mouthful of grass. Behind and ahead of them, the road stretched away, empty, the woods on either side.

When at last they came to another log house with a woman chasing chickens away from her pumpkin patch, Nell asked the way to Woodville.

"You want to go east," the woman told her. "Back where you've come from. You'll never make it before sundown."

Nell was so downcast, she couldn't hide her misery. The woman came closer. Nell was torn between telling her everything and keeping a wary silence.

"You have anything to eat there?" the woman asked her.

Nell shook her head. Her stomach ached from green apples and raw corn.

"Turn your horse around in my barnyard and wait," the woman told her. "I'll be right back."

Nell turned and then set the horse back on the road in case they had to make a quick getaway.

The woman brought Nell two slabs of bread, one spread with bacon fat, the other with molasses. Thanking her, Nell set off at once, gobbling the two pieces of bread one after the other. The dark came quickly, the trees seeming to crowd in on the road and forcing her to stop until daybreak. Nell chafed at the darkness and was urging the horse on again at the first light of morning. She measured her progress by landmarks she recognized, until at last she came to a stretch of road she didn't know at all.

Mile after mile, the horse kept up his big, easy stride, but Nell was so worried about the time she had lost, she was sure he was slowing down. When the first real houses appeared, she didn't dare to believe they meant the town was close. Then she came to a bridge, and after it a steep-roofed building with a sign on it for paints and oils. There were people about, work sounds and wheels turning. Was that a church steeple up ahead? Then where were the railroad tracks, the depot?

Nell tightened the reins to let another wagon by. The man driving and the two boys with him passed so close, she might have touched them.

"Big load for a little girl," the man commented with a smile.

"It's the horse that's pulling," Nell answered. "Will I come to the flour mill?"

"Just on a bit. Over to the right."

The two boys stared, one of them twisting around as the wagons drew apart. Now that the other wagon was on its way, Nell was sorry she hadn't asked the man about the Fowlers, too.

She halted the horse and wagon beside a hayrick piled high with corn. Then she slid to the ground. Two men stood just inside the big door to the mill shouting at each other, although neither sounded angry. Nell guessed the man with the yellowy dust all over him was the miller. His eyebrows looked like furry caterpillars.

Seeing her, he shouted, "Stay out! Don't want you caught in them gears." He turned back to the other man.

She had no intention of setting foot inside with the tremendous clatter and din going on. She tugged on his floury sleeve.

"I said," the miller told her, "outside. Your dad will have to wait his turn."

Tears sprang to her eyes. He couldn't hear her and wouldn't be bothered, and soon it would be too dark to find her way. Trudging back to the horse, she took hold of his bridle and pressed her face against his long, bony nose.

"Well, then?" said a deep voice. The miller stood over her, but she could see him eyeing the horse, the sweat marks and the grime.

"Do you remember him?" she asked. "Do you remember the man who drove him here the other day?" Was it two days ago or three? Letting go of the bridle, she described with her hands a deep brim around her own head. "He had a black hat." She didn't know what to say about Joe's left hand.

"Oh, yes," the miller replied, "the Indian."

Indian! Were they speaking of the same man? "He works for Mr. and Mrs. Fowler," she added. She needed to lean against the horse's head again, only it wasn't there. She was drifting in a floury haze. Then she felt herself taken by the elbows. She was sitting on the ground, the big horse blowing into her hair, questions coming at her from the miller and the other man, and now a woman as well. Nell tried to explain about waiting at the bridge over Musquash Stream, about the robbers, about being lost.

The miller said, "That Indian's not from around here. I don't even know his name."

The other man said, "I wouldn't trust an Indian with my horse, never mind all that wagon load."

The woman said, "Dinner first."

Nell was afraid to let the horse out of her sight, but the miller rummaged around at the back of the wagon, returned with a halter and rope, and began to unbuckle straps and unhook a chain. The miller shook his head as the horse stepped free of the shafts. With the harness off, its print remained as a black crust.

"Come along," the miller's wife said to Nell. "It's not just the horse that needs a wash."

Inside the kitchen parlor the sudden warmth was dizzying. Nell clutched the table. The miller's wife filled a basin with water from a steaming kettle. She set out a jar of soft soap and a flannel.

"I don't mean to put you out," Nell murmured.

"It's you I should put out," the woman told her. "In the laundry yard."

Nell dipped the flannel cloth in the basin and then held it to her face. How good it felt.

"Needs more than that," the miller's wife declared. She unbuttoned Nell's blouse only to find beneath it a jumper and beneath that a petticoat. "So many layers!" she exclaimed. She parted Nell's hair, examined it closely, and then scrubbed it with the soapy flannel. After that Nell washed herself while the miller's wife dished stew into a bowl and set it before Nell. "Be careful," she warned. "It's been on the stove since dinner, so it's a mite warm. Here's cider to help it down."

Nell drank from the mug. Looking at the stew, she said, "I have no money."

"I don't keep an inn," the miller's wife responded. "Friends and travelers never leave here hungry."

Nell dipped her spoon into the bowl. "I came here hungry," she gasped after the first delicious mouthful. After that she ate more slowly. In between bites she told the miller's wife about Louisa going to people named Warburton near Woodville. If no one here knew the Fowlers, said Nell, she ought to go to the Warburtons. They would have some idea where the Fowlers lived, because the Home had made sure that each family knew about the other.

The miller's wife said that her husband would be able to direct Nell to the Warburtons. By and by she would speak to him about it.

The hot food and the indoor warmth weighed down on Nell until her head rested on the table. She was barely aware of the spoon being pried from her hand. Then she was left in peace.

Sometime later the miller's wife prodded her. Nell would have to leave now if she hoped to reach the Warburton farm before nightfall. Nell rubbed her eyes and then finished buttoning her clothes.

Going outside was a shock. The end of the day had turned cold and gray. It was hard to think of setting out again. There was the horse, though, harnessed and hitched. He'd had a good feed, too, the miller told Nell, and there was an extra bundle of hay shoved under the rubber blanket.

She listened with care as he described the fork at the sawmills that would take her up Mugaleep Mountain. It was steep and hard; she must be sure not to stop, or the horse might not make it. Just when she began to glimpse the open land going down the other side, she would come to an even rougher road running along the ridge.

"Soon as you take it there on your right, you begin to look for one of the clearings from the logging roads. Don't drive too far in. Hitch the horse to a tree where the ground is level and walk the rest of the way. Only farm there is Warburtons'." He lifted her up onto the wagon seat. "Be careful coming back, too. Keep slow." Then he added, "You positive about the Warburtons?"

There was something unsettling about the way he asked, especially now, after all the directions.

"Pretty sure," she said.

Frowning, he exchanged a look with his wife.

"It's a surprise," he remarked as he slapped the horse on the rump to start him off. "Of course, I don't know them that well. Just not the kind of people you think of taking in a Home child." He rubbed his face, and a cloud of creamy dust swirled up.

Nell couldn't see his expression. Then she had to pay attention to the horse and to others on the road. All she could do was call her thanks as she waved over her shoulder.

4/Mugaleep Mountain

Driving through Woodville, Nell imagined living in a house with a fence around it like one up the side road, with drooping sunflower stalks and lacy asters gone to seed. Think of having neighbors like the miller and his wife. But the great mounds of chips and sawdust on the other side of town hemmed in her view of the road and the river that curved alongside it. The din of the sawmills was so deafening, it was a relief to turn onto the mountain road, at least until the woods took over from the homesteads and cabins.

The horse bent to the climb, ignoring the squirrels that darted in front of him and the birds that dropped from branches to peck in the dirt kicked loose by his hooves. The wagon shook and rattled over the deep ruts and washouts. Nell held tight to the seat and wondered how long they would have to travel this way without a sign of human life.

The horse seemed to sense a change when they neared the ridge. He was eager to take the narrower road to the right. Then he stopped abruptly. Nell turned to see what he was looking at and found herself gazing into the great soft eyes of a cow that had come up behind the wagon and was licking flour dust from the rubber blanket. Three more cows emerged from the uphill side and milled about. Another came lumbering from the other direction. Shaking its head as if to charge the horse, it veered off at the last moment and raised a wet nose to the flour dust, too.

At the same moment that two other cows broke through the undergrowth, Nell heard and then saw Louisa plunging down a narrow track between the trees. Her skirt was snagged by blackberry canes, her curls stuck with twigs and tree moss. She was flailing a big stick and bawling at the top of her lungs.

"Louisa!" Nell shouted.

Louisa kept on howling and flinging the stick from side to side. Nell slid to the ground and then felt very small with all those cows so close. Running to meet Louisa, she reached out to grab her arms. It was the only way Nell knew how to quiet her when she was raging like this.

Louisa gulped and stared.

"What's wrong?" Nell asked her. "Why are you crying?"

"It's my fault," Louisa gasped. "I can't make the gate stay shut. He said this time . . . this time not to come back without them."

"Without the cows? All right, we'll do it together." Taking the stick, Nell swished it at the heads of nearby cows.

"Not that way." Louisa began to wail. "They'll go down the mountain. They can't get past the wagon."

"All right, all right. I'll move the wagon. I'm supposed to tie the horse in a logging road."

Louisa pointed to a clearing just ahead, but it was hard to lead the horse away from the cows.

"Hurry," sobbed Louisa.

As soon as Nell got the horse and wagon off the road, she ran back to help Louisa. But for every cow they got heading in the right direction, there was another that wheeled and took off toward the mountain road.

Racing back and forth, the two girls finally managed to get all the cows in a long ambling stream that began to flow in the proper direction.

Following along behind them, Nell told Louisa all about Joe and the robbers. But Louisa's mind was still caught up in her private misery, and she didn't seem to take in anything Nell said until she mentioned having to feed the horse and settle him for the night. At that point Louisa informed Nell that as soon as the cows were closed in, she would be ready to go.

"Go where?" Nell asked in surprise.

"With you," Louisa said.

"But I just came. I have to . . . I can't take you."

Louisa just tramped on, a little cowlike herself as she slouched and swung her arms from side to side.

Nell explained again that she needed to speak to Mr. or Mrs. Warburton to learn the way to Mrs. Fowler.

Just then the cows surged ahead. Louisa said, "They're hungry. They'll go in now because they think they'll be fed. When there isn't any," she went on bleakly, "they'll try to push out again."

As soon as the cows turned off the little road, Nell could see the log house, and the barn and shed below it. The cows nudged one another at the gate.

Louisa said to Nell, "Don't come nearer."

"Why not?"

"Don't you come," Louisa warned. "Wait here."

Since it was nearly dark, Nell worried about finding her way back to the horse and wagon. It was cold standing there on the ridge. What was taking Louisa so long? Nell tucked her fingers under her shawl. By now the Warburtons should have called her inside.

When she could wait no longer, Nell made her way down to the log house and peered through a window. She saw a man seated at a table, a woman serving him. She didn't see Louisa.

Nell didn't know what to do. She recalled Louisa's warning plea and kept very still. Then she caught sight of a crack of light around the barn door. Moving almost soundlessly toward it, she heard a creak and a rustle from inside the barn.

"Ssh!"

"Louisa?"

"Yes, ssh. I was going to get you after they finish supper. Did they see you?"

"No." Nell's nose prickled with the fumes from sodden bedding and manure. The lamp hung near a pen full of young pigs lying heaped on one another. "Are you hiding?" Nell whispered. "Don't you want your supper?"

"No supper," Louisa answered. "Because of the cows getting out. But there's potatoes and squashes here. They're all right. I had some last night."

"Last night?" Nell exclaimed. "Why?"

"I forgot to stir the soap. I spoiled the batch she was making."

"When do they let you in the house? Where do you sleep?"

Louisa nodded toward the ladder. "Up in the hay. It's because I get everything wrong."

"Never mind," Nell told her, "I'll show you what to do. I'll explain to Mr. and Mrs. Warburton that you need time to learn."

Louisa didn't respond to that. She just dug into a barrel and came up with two handfuls of potatoes.

"We'll keep track of what I eat," Nell went on. "Otherwise, it's stealing."

Louisa emptied the potatoes in Nell's skirt and then made a pouch of her own. Even in the dim lamplight Nell could recognize the set of Louisa's mouth, glum and determined. Laden with potatoes and squash, and with the lamp to light their way, they trudged along the ridge road until the horse heard them and began to neigh. Terrified that the Warburtons would hear him, Louisa ran stumbling ahead. Trying to keep the tiny blob of light in sight, Nell tripped and nearly lost her skirtful of vegetables. By now the horse was quiet. Then Louisa cried out.

"What is it?" Nell called to her.

"My potatoes." Louisa was struggling to yank up the horse's head. "He's eating my potatoes."

"Never mind," Nell told her breathlessly. "He's hungry, too. We have plenty here." She fetched hay from the rear of the wagon while Louisa munched hungrily on a raw potato. Nell bit into one, too. It was gritty and cold against her teeth. Without mentioning the stew she had eaten that afternoon, she told Louisa she wasn't hungry and gave the potato to her to finish.

The girls settled under the rubber sheet with the buffalo robe wrapped around them. Nell tried to warm Louisa's icy hands and asked her whether she had remembered to tell Mrs. Warburton about the lost gloves. Louisa shook her head.

"I'll tell her tomorrow," Nell promised. She would also remind Louisa about speaking plainly and politely so that Mrs. Warburton would understand her. "Everything will be all right," Nell finished.

"No," said Louisa. "Never."

Nell blew on Louisa's stiff fingers. Tomorrow morning was soon enough to set Louisa straight. If Nell tried to persuade her tonight, she would only have to repeat herself the next day. She would have to be careful, too. If she came right out and told Louisa that this was her last chance to be placed near Nell, Louisa might retreat into silence and shut herself away even from Nell.

Nell often wondered about the place Louisa went to when she couldn't face her life. Nell imagined a kind of underwater dimness with everything blurred and slow. What was it like to be beyond the reach of everyday voices and ways? How could Nell keep Louisa from sinking?

"Anyway," Nell whispered to Louisa, "we're together again for a little while."

"I knew you'd come," Louisa said. "It's what I prayed for."

5/Hiding

Louisa's steps squeaked and crunched over the frost-struck ground. She was in a hurry to get to the barn ahead of Mr. Warburton. She insisted that Nell stay behind.

When the sun rose and the twigs and pods slipped their fragile casings of ice, everything dripped and shone. Nell took the horse for a drink at a tiny mountain stream. Along the way he browsed on wet bushes and cropped the heads off weeds. Some of the seeds and stalks must have tasted bitter, because every once in a while he tossed his head and mouthed the chewed stuff out.

Nell wondered what the Home had written to prepare the Warburtons for Louisa. She hoped they didn't know too much about Louisa's failure at Dr. Satterlee's. For months the girls had worked side by side and shared the attic bed. It was only after Nell started to attend school that Louisa had become unmanageable. School for Nell would take less than three months out of the whole year. But Louisa's tantrums upset the doctor's patients. The girls were returned to the Home.

If this place didn't work out, either, where would the Home send Louisa next? It wasn't likely to be near Nell. It might be far away.

After the horse had fed on weeds and acorns, Nell tied him at a fresh spot in the clearing and walked to the farm. She stayed well back on the ridge road and waited. There wasn't a sign of life. She thought about the room she had seen last night. There had been a table and a stove. There had been food. She imagined a pan of leftover porridge and maybe a bit of pork from breakfast. But she knew she couldn't just march into an empty kitchen and help herself. As it was, last night's potatoes and squash must be reckoned as a debt to be paid.

The only thing to do was find Mrs. Warburton, explain herself and Louisa, and learn the way to the Fowler farm. If Mrs. Warburton offered her a meal the way the miller's wife had, Nell would gratefully accept it. Otherwise she would be on her way.

She followed the ridge road until the woods opened downhill. Two oxen stood at a fence, looking into a hay field where a man and a woman and Louisa were raking and piling hay. Nell was about to call out to them when she saw the man, who must be Mr. Warburton, yank Louisa's arm so hard that her head snapped back and forth. He was shouting at her, too, but Nell couldn't make out the words. Then he bundled hay in Louisa's arms so high that she couldn't see in front of her. When she lost her balance, she dumped the hay and scrambled to pick it up again. But Mr. Warburton was striding back to her. He took her arm again; this time he flung her toward the field below.

As Louisa tumbled, staggered up, and then ran, Nell took off downhill toward the hay field. But she stopped short of revealing herself, and crouched behind a boulder. The man and woman continued to work. The sky darkened. They looked up, and then hustled away without a backward or downhill glance.

As soon as they were gone, Nell crossed the field to the one below, where Louisa was spading potatoes. "I'll help you until they come back," Nell said to her.

"They won't come if it rains hard," Louisa said. She tossed aside a potato cut by the spade.

"What do you do with the broken ones?" Nell asked as she scooped whole ones into a burlap sack.

"Hide them. Eat them. He says I must pay for every one I spoil."

Nell worked silently, mulling over the problem of finding her way to the Fowler farm if she couldn't speak to Mr. or Mrs. Warburton. A fine drizzle clung like silver down to her sleeves and shawl, but her hands and skirt were already creased with mud. The drizzle bore down on them. Louisa sat back on her heels, rubbed a split potato on her skirt, and munched grittily. "Mr. Warburton says he hopes Mr. Fowler got a better girl than me."

Nell tried to wipe the mud from Louisa's mouth but only smeared on more from her own fingers. "I knew he'd be able to tell me how to find Mrs. Fowler. Probably he has a letter from the Home that says where the Fowlers live. If you could find the letter, I wouldn't need to ask him."

Louisa sent her a look of despair. "How can I? I'm not even allowed inside."

"You will be." The rain was falling steadily now, drenching and cold. "You'll work so hard and be so good, with me helping you, that they'll take pity."

Louisa looked doubtful.

"Don't you see, Louisa? You have to. Just as soon as I see that letter and find out how to get to the Fowler farm, I can tell Mrs. Fowler all about you here, and then she'll do something."

"Do what?"

"I don't know," Nell said truthfully. "But I'm sure she'll help. Anyway," she added, "I do see that I'd better stay hidden. You were right about that, Louisa."

They worked on, their skirts dragging and clinging, their stockings torn and their knees raw.

"I'll need more food for the horse," Nell said.

Louisa nodded. "Save one of the sacks. There's oats in the barn."

"I'll have to reckon how much of their food I've used."

"You're working for it."

Nell pondered that. Could she take potatoes and oats and other things in payment for work the Warburtons knew nothing about? Whatever she did here in secret would seem to them to be due to a reformed Louisa. That's what Nell was aiming at. "I'll just keep track," she murmured, already planning to stash some of the damaged potatoes behind the big boulder above the hay field.

Louisa started to haul the full sacks to the barn. Nell dragged them as far as the ox field; she didn't dare get closer to the barn. It was hard work, the sacks bumping over the rough ground, snagging on roots and lodging behind rocks.

"Think how pleased Mr. Warburton will be," Nell said, trying to encourage Louisa.

But Louisa just staggered along, too miserable to care.

That night Nell was too filthy to sleep on the cornmeal and flour, so she crawled under the wagon instead, with the buffalo robe for warmth. In the morning a pale watery sunlight filtered through the trees. Nell washed her clothes in the stream and put on her clean, dry things. She shook out the buffalo robe as best she could, and hung it on a branch. She decided to stick close to the clearing while everything was drying. That way, if she heard anyone coming, she could fling her belongings onto the wagon and take right off.

Later in the day when everything was packed away again, Nell went back to the Warburton farm. Everyone was working in the potato field. Louisa had a wooden yoke across her shoulders with sacks tied to each end. She staggered under her load as she headed for the barn.

Nell ran back along the ridge and then down to the barn to meet her.

"There's cheese for you, and bread," Louisa told her as she stooped to unload the sacks. "In the oat bin."

"Why do you have that thing on your shoulders?" Nell asked her.

"To keep the potatoes from being smashed on the ground."

"What about the letter?"

Louisa shook her head. Nell saw she was still wearing yesterday's clothes, caked with mud. That meant she hadn't been taken inside yet. At least she had been given bread and cheese, enough for her to put some aside for Nell. Maybe Louisa was too dirty now to be allowed in the house.

"Tonight we'll get you cleaned up," Nell said. "You'll feel better. They'll like you better."

Louisa rubbed her shoulder where the yoke pressed. "I have to go," she said, "or he'll switch me."

Nell considered going inside for a look right now. But she was terrified of being caught. She gulped down the bread and cheese and then filled her sack with oats and hay for the horse. She knew he had been in the harness much too long and that it must be rubbing cruelly, the way the yoke had rubbed Louisa. So Nell took the horse grazing by the stream and spent the rest of the afternoon scrubbing wherever she could reach under the collar and harness saddle. He wasn't the least disturbed by her sitting up there on his back. Intent on foraging in the undergrowth as far as the wagon allowed, he moved about unhurriedly, sometimes leaning into the pressure of her hands.

The next day the Warburtons and Louisa were back in the hay field turning the wet hay. Nell ducked inside the barn to check the oat bin for more bread and cheese. Her groping fingers flicked paper as they closed around a crust. Her spirits soared. Louisa must have found a letter from the Home. If only it had the information Nell needed.

Taking it to the light, she skimmed the words until she came to the name Fowler: "Mr. and Mrs. Gabriel Fowler, over by Upper Medet." Upper Medet, that was it! Nell must have been so close when she spoke to those children in Medet Settlement. She read on: "Mrs. Fowler has just come from Maine and knows few people in the area, so her girl is for companionship as well as work. She has kindly waited for us to find a place not too distant for the bigger girl, whom you will find on the dull side but able to carry out many tasks expected of boys."

The rest of the letter was about the terms, about caring for the child as if she were one of their own. Modest payment was to be set aside until Louisa was ready to leave and live on her own. Nell leaned against the barn and tipped her face to the sun. How unfair it was. No one could know how Louisa was being used here. How could she stay in a place like this?

Hearing voices approach, Nell scrambled out of the way and up to the ridge. Upper Medet. The sooner she got there, the sooner something could be done for Louisa. Nell would leave as soon as she had a chance to say good-bye to Louisa and reassure her.

In her excitement over the letter, Nell had forgotten the bread, so she shared the oats with the horse. After so many raw potatoes, they were a welcome change. They lasted longer, too.

Still hoping to be on her way before dark, Nell went back toward the farm. She could hear some commotion behind the barn, but she had to go all the way around through the ox field before she caught sight of Louisa with the yoked oxen. The beasts were plodding around and around in a circle; Louisa was swatting them with a long stick. Mystified, Nell crept closer. Now she could see that the oxen were dragging the end of a pole that was attached to one that went up and down and led through an opening into a shed. As soon as Mrs. Warburton appeared, Nell ducked behind that shed.

"Keep them going," Mrs. Warburton told Louisa. "It's got to be smooth."

Nell peeked around the corner of the shed in time to see Louisa stop to brush flies from her face. Mrs. Warburton snatched the stick and whacked first the oxen and then Louisa, who cried out.

"You shilly-shally," Mrs. Warburton warned, "and you'll get it just like all the other dumb animals. You hear?"

Louisa swung at the oxen. They lurched.

"Not like that," railed Mrs. Warburton. "You mind me or you'll be sorry." She stomped off into the shed.

Spinning out of the way, Nell backed into hens scratching in manure. While they squawked and shrilled, she cowered, certain that Mrs. Warburton would come out and discover her. But nothing happened. Mrs. Warburton clanked pails inside the shed, the oxen tramped their tight circle, and the hens went muttering off.

Keeping low, Nell scrambled away from the barnyard and out through the field to the road. She was just passing the farm along the ridge when Louisa cried out again. This time the cry exploded into shrieks that sent shivers up and down Nell's back. Mrs. Warburton, sounding annoyed, called to Mr. Warburton, but Nell saw no one. She ducked down, waiting to learn what had happened to Louisa, but all was silent now. There was nothing else Nell could do but keep on waiting.

At sundown Nell moved the horse and wagon closer to the mountain road. She folded Louisa's dry things, stared at them briefly, and then tucked them under the rubber blanket. So that was that. She would take Louisa to Mrs. Fowler. In the Home it had been drilled into the children that running away was like stealing. Nell, as well as Louisa, would be stealing from the Warburtons. Nell shook off that thought. What mattered was getting Louisa away from Mugaleep Mountain.

The trouble was that now it was too dark to leave. And when would Louisa come? Even as Nell wondered and worried, she heard Louisa sobbing and babbling.

"Over here," Nell called. "I'm here."

Louisa's lamp bobbed and dipped as she limped toward Nell.

"What happened to you?" Nell cried. "What took you so long?"

"The ox," Louisa said through her tears. "He was on my foot. It hurts to walk. And then you weren't there."

"Oh, Louisa." Nell hugged her. "I moved the horse nearer the road."

"I thought you were gone. Found out where to go and went."

"I didn't. I wouldn't. See, here's the horse. Right here."

Louisa shrank from him.

"He won't hurt you. He's going to take us away first thing in the morning."

"No," sobbed Louisa. "Now. We have to go now."

"We can't. Not in the dark. It's too steep. Louisa, stop crying and listen. You can get right up on the wagon and stay there."

Whimpering with pain, Louisa hauled herself up and crawled under the buffalo robe. Nell blew out the lamp and carried it up with her. Something else she was stealing, something more to reckon as a debt.

Had the devil lured her into a life of crime the way they had warned about in the Home? She hadn't really noticed him leading her on. Why didn't she feel different?

Too anxious to sleep, Nell wondered how long it would take before the Warburtons realized Louisa was gone. Would they care enough to come looking for her? Nell had no idea. She told herself it didn't matter. She would already have Louisa miles away. Anyhow, the slow oxen would be no match for the horse.

Moaning in her sleep, Louisa turned on her side and whimpered again. Nell stared into the darkness, willing the night to end. Already she thought she could see the first glimmer of dawn.

6/"Seize Her!"

Every time the wheels hit a stone or rut, Louisa let out a cry of pain from behind.

"It'll be smoother soon," Nell kept promising. What mattered was keeping the horse centered as the road plunged. If only there were more light. It was as though daybreak had stalled, leaving just a sullen spread of gray through the trees.

The wagon seemed to be a goad propelling the horse downhill; soon the trees on either side were a mere blur. Nell would have called up Louisa to help her haul in the reins, but Louisa was howling in her agony.

"Hush!" Nell shouted at her. "Stop that noise."

"It hurts, it hurts," cried Louisa.

"Someone will hear you. Listen, Louisa, we're nearly there." Was that true? Nell was almost sure that the trees were thinning. Here was a cabin, a tiny homestead. They hurtled past so fast, it might have been imagined. Bracing her feet and leaning back, Nell pulled the reins with all her might. "Hide," she yelled at Louisa. "Pull the blanket right over you, so if anyone sees me they won't know you're here."

"I can't. Help!"

Swiveling, Nell's feet slipped. The reins flew up. At the same moment the wagon swerved and somewhere ahead a voice shouted, "Seize her!"

The horse, stiff-gaited at the turn, brought them out onto the main road. Mist swirled up from the river, wrapping the mounds of sawdust, even the sawmills, in white vapor. Nell couldn't see anyone at all. Who would be lying in wait like this at the break of day? The robbers searching for their loot? The police?

"Seize her! Whoa!"

The horse stopped short, jarring the wagon. A muffled cry came from the back.

Trying to cover Louisa's voice with her own, Nell shouted, "Get out of my way!" But there was someone at the horse's head. It looked like a boy, but she couldn't be sure in the mist. She could feel him grab the horse's rein at the bit. She yanked back, but the leather was pulled right out of her hand.

And now Nell saw him walking up to her. Yes, a boy. Only a boy. What kind of threat could he possibly be?

In an instant he was up on the seat and pushing her rudely aside. He had the reins. She tried to snatch them from him, but he was bigger and stronger.

"I'm driving," he informed her. "Sit still."

"You can't," she told him. "I'll scream. The miller knows me. He'll stop you."

"If you scream," the boy told her, "you'll wake the whole town of Woodville and they'll put you in jail for taking off with Jessie Fowler's horse and wagon."

Nell gasped. "You know her?"

The boy's eyes were on the road. "I know who you are, too. Nell Haskins. You never came when you should, and now it's too late."

That's what Joe had said. But how could she be too late? "I'll make it up to Mrs. Fowler. I will."

The boy cast her a disgusted glance. "I doubt it. She left yesterday. Gave up."

"She's not in Upper Medet?" Nell's mouth went dry. She could hardly get the words out. "Where did she go? Why?"

"To her family in Maine. She couldn't stay the winter with Gabe Fowler gone and without all the flour and corn and without her horse and wagon, too. Besides, the neighbors kept telling her she'd never see those things again."

Woodville was still asleep as they passed through it. Nell

scarcely noticed the houses. She didn't bother to seek out the depot or the mill. All she could think about was Mrs. Fowler giving
up on her. "But I'll write her," she declared. She turned to the
boy. "Are you her son?"

Grinning at the suggestion, he said, "If I was, I guess she
wouldn't hurry away so fast. She felt awful."

"But it wasn't my fault. You don't know what happened."

"I know some," the boy told her. "I've been to see the miller. I
was coming to look for you up Mugaleep Mountain, but it got
dark." He paused as a dog came running into the road barking at
them. When it fell back from the wagon, he went on. "I'm Peter.
Peter Mussel. Grandfather and me, we work for the Fowlers. Or
did."

Nell shook her head. "But Mrs. Fowler will come back now,
won't she?"

Peter shrugged. "Maybe she'll stay on with her folks now. Until
her baby comes, anyway." They were leaving town, the wheels
rumbling over the bridge. "The neighbors brought us to Woodville. They kept telling her she'd never see Joe Pennowit again.
That's my grandfather. They said Indians steal . . . steal children.
Jessie Fowler was so worried for you, worried sick."

Nell sighed. "I'm so sorry. I wish she'd gone to the miller."

"She did, only he was busy inside the mill, and the Cartwrights—those are the neighbors—they needed to get her things
down to the depot. So they took her to see the minister. She was
feeling so bad, they left us there. They had to get back home. So
we didn't get over to the mill again. I mean, I did, only it was after
her train went."

"We need to send a letter right away to stop her worrying," Nell
said.

"You can do that. I have to go look for Grandfather. He must
be hurt bad or he'd be home. He can find his way anywhere in the
woods."

It was hard for Nell to think of this boy as the grandson of an

Indian. He wasn't dark-skinned. His eyes were gray. He looked like any other fast-growing boy, his wrists practically bursting from his sleeves.

"Did Mrs. Fowler leave you in charge?" she asked him.

He nodded. "But I'm not bound to stay if I can find work closer to town. If I leave, I'm to close up the house and take the stock to the Cartwrights for the winter."

Nell regarded him doubtfully. It sounded like a lot of responsibility for a boy. "How old are you?" she asked him.

"Nearly thirteen. I can be on my own."

Nell wondered why Mrs. Fowler trusted him when she didn't trust his grandfather. Peter caught her looking at him. He must have guessed what she was thinking, because he said, "I'm mostly not Indian." Then he added, "It was Gabe Fowler took us on. We all got along real well."

They went on for a while in silence, each mulling over what had happened and what had seemed to happen. When they took an uphill fork and the road worsened, Nell began to worry about Louisa. She was bound to cry out again. Even if her voice was muffled, Peter would surely hear her.

"How much longer?" Nell asked him.

"A while yet. We're trying the shortcut. I don't know as the horse can make it, though. You seem to have run him pretty hard."

"I did the best I could," Nell retorted. "I had to learn a lot all at once."

"Well, the way you were driving, you're lucky you didn't lose a wheel. I'll teach you how to handle a horse."

Nell said stiffly, "I'll wait for Mrs. Fowler to teach me."

"If she comes," he replied. Then he added, "If she doesn't, I can't imagine what I'm to do with you. Mrs. Fowler was sure you were gone for good. I never expected a girl on my hands."

Nell drew a breath. "Girls."

He didn't miss a beat. "But it won't be for long. I know I'll find Grandfather."

"Girls," Nell repeated. "Two girls." She saw his neck cords tighten. His face went red. "Please don't mind," she said to him. "We had to. She had to get away."

"You're teasing." His voice was thick with anger. "You don't mean it."

With the wagon jouncing her, Nell had to kneel as she leaned way over to pull the rubber blanket aside. The buffalo robe was pushed into a bundle. Louisa huddled beside it, drenched in sweat.

After one glance Peter turned for a better look. "She's sick?"

"The ox stepped on her foot."

"We need Grandfather," he muttered. "We need his medicine bag. I don't know what to do about this kind of trouble."

Nell tried to explain to him about the Warburtons. But Peter just went on muttering about all the trouble they were in. Nell could tell from the way he sat hunched away from her that he didn't want to be bothered with any kind of hard-luck story. Yet the way he clenched his hands into fists, gripping the reins as if for dear life, showed Nell that he couldn't help hearing, couldn't help being bothered. He was bothered even more than he would admit.

7/Seesur

The first thing Peter did when they reached the Fowler farm was slosh water all over the horse.

"Poor Seesur," he declared, rubbing at the sweat marks.

"Seesur?" Nell, who was trying to coax Louisa down from the wagon, was brought up short. "Is that the horse's name?"

"Why would I call him Seesur if it wasn't?"

So Peter hadn't been shouting "Seize her!" at the bottom of Mugaleep Mountain. "You mean, S-E-E-S-U-R?" she spelled.

"I suppose so. I'm not too good at spelling. He's named for an ancient emperor. That's what Gabe told me."

Nell turned her attention back to Louisa. "I'll get you something to eat. You'll feel better then." She asked Peter if there was something inside the house she might cook for their supper. None of them had eaten all day, and Nell had had only oats the night before.

"Beans in the crock, ham and bacon hanging up above, vegetables in the root cellar." He nodded toward a mound at the side of the log house.

"Can I go in?"

"Go anywhere," he told her dismissively. "I've got stock to feed." He led Seesur away to the barn.

Nell tiptoed as she walked through the door. It was like starting a new book. A book about herself, she thought, not about a Home child but about Nell, who was the Fowlers' girl.

She crossed the kitchen-parlor to the doorway on the right and saw a big bed with a pretty coverlet, bright curtains at the tiny window, a chest, a nightstand, and a beautiful new cradle. Turning, her eyes swept the main room. There was the stove, the wood box beside it, and here the crock with dried beans, matches on the shelf, and a jug of water. There was a half wall in the far corner and another door leading to a small indoor shed with a stone sink.

Eventually she had a fire started. She scooped some beans into a pot with water to start cooking. But they would take a long time. Everyone needed to eat now. Turning once more, she caught sight of a basket of eggs on the sideboard. The frying pan hung from a nail below it. All she needed now were potatoes to make a good fry, so she went to the root cellar. She managed to yank the tiny, sloping door open under the mound of turf, but then she had to grope blindly in one barrel after another. She ended up with parsnips, which she had thought were carrots, and potatoes.

Back in the kitchen, she cooked up a batch of potatoes and parsnips in lard she found in a jar, because she couldn't reach the bacon hanging overhead. When they were well done, she added more lard and as many eggs as she could fit in the pan. Then she called Peter in.

For the first time he gave her a fleeting look of approval. They ate together out of the pan, taking turns until she reminded him about Louisa. They went on eating but left a decent portion for Nell to carry to the wagon.

But Louisa wasn't hungry, only thirsty. Nell coaxed her into eating a few forkfuls before she turned her face away. It was flushed and puffy. Her eyes were very bright.

Louisa asked about the privy, but by the time Peter and Nell got her down from the wagon, it was dark and trouble enough just bringing her into the house. "We'll find a chamber pot under the bed, I'm sure," Nell whispered.

Peter said, "You will. We don't have one in the wood-house chamber because of getting it down the ladder."

Nell felt too shy to respond. She was able to turn her full attention to Louisa, who sagged between them and tried to keep her hugely swollen foot from touching anything.

Once Louisa was on the bed, Nell and Peter had a close look at the foot in the lamplight. The stocking was stretched tighter than skin and could hardly be peeled off. Louisa made a choking sound way back in her throat but didn't actually cry. For the first time Nell was really alarmed.

Out in the kitchen-parlor she talked with Peter about going to the neighbors for help. He reminded her that the Cartwrights were busybodies and likely to go straight off to the Warburtons.

"What if Louisa needs a doctor?" Nell asked him.

He had no answer. They faced each other, each taking some measure of the other's position.

"Could you bring her to someone else?" She thought of the children of Medet Settlement.

"I'll be off looking for Grandfather."

"Doesn't Mrs. Fowler keep medicine here?"

"She gives molasses tea for a cough," he said. "You could try that."

Nell was stumped. If that was the best they could do for Louisa, they'd better try it.

After drinking from the cup Nell held for her, Louisa dropped off to sleep.

"She's already better," Nell announced, wanting to believe it. She pawed through the basket of carrots and onions Peter had fetched from the cellar. She might start simmering a soup for Louisa if Peter would cut off a bit of the ham to go in the pot.

He nodded but continued to sit at the table, his chin in his hands.

"Something else," he said. "Something else you better know."

"What?"

"Those men, those robbers, I think they're the same men who came here looking for work at the logging camp. Grandfather stopped Gabe hiring them. He said he knew one of them from long ago and he was trouble. He did something bad."

"To your grandfather?"

Peter gave a tremendous yawn that all but swallowed his words. "Don't know. He wouldn't talk about it. He just made Gabe Fowler send them away. They looked plenty mean when they left."

Nell guessed that Peter had been figuring all this out for some time. Now that he had reached the conclusion that those men were out to get his grandfather more than the horse and wagon, he was even more anxious to go looking for him.

"Don't worry," she said. "If he knows his way around these woods, he could be hiding."

Mumbling "Suppose so," Peter nodded. Then his head dropped to the table, his arm sprawling and nearly knocking over Louisa's empty cup.

After washing up, Nell went into the bedroom. For a while she lay on her back feeling the heat that came from Louisa and trying to think of doctoring ways she must have heard about at Dr. Satterlee's. Bromides were good for stomach trouble, she remembered. Would they help with a fever as well? And how was she to find any?

Maybe by tomorrow Louisa would be better. Nell would wash the foot and find something clean for a bandage. And she would brush the snarls out of Louisa's hair. That always made her feel better.

So much to do tomorrow. Nell would have to find a way of writing a letter to Mrs. Fowler. Then she would need to get it posted. She was mulling over how to explain about Louisa when she heard the outside door open and close. Was Peter leaving now, in the middle of the night? Maybe he was just going out to the privy. She lay very still, listening for his return. Someone spoke in a low voice.

Nell's first thought was that the robbers had come looking for

Joe. Her second, that the nosy neighbors were checking up on Peter, made more sense. What if they found Louisa?

Nell slipped off the bed, dragging the coverlet with her and wrapping herself in it as she stood at the door.

Peter spoke, his tone blunted by sleep. "Why didn't you come right back?"

There was a lilt of a question in the soft-spoken response.

Nell pressed the latch down; the door creaked open. There sat Peter at the table. Beyond the lamplight stood a man, who turned quickly, his face still shadowed. Nell guessed that he was staring at her.

"Here," he exclaimed, but still in an undertone. "You're all right?"

She couldn't recognize the voice, but she knew it was Joe, Peter's grandfather.

"Come to the light," he ordered.

Clutching the coverlet and nearly tripping on it, she slithered over to the table. "Are you all right?" she echoed.

"All right and not all right," he replied.

"What kind of answer is that?" Peter demanded, his voice frayed. "All this time, not knowing."

His grandfather said, "I thought they have girl. Have her somewhere. How can I come without her?" He moved to the stove. "Cook supper now. Talk tomorrow."

"There's beans," Nell said, "only they're not done yet. Shall I cook some vegetables?"

But he already had the ham down from the rafter. Pulling a knife from his belt, he sliced once, and a slab of ham flipped onto the table. Now she could see him, his clothes slick with grime, the knife looking more like a weapon than a tool.

He uncovered the bean pot, sniffed, and replaced the cover. "Need pork and molasses," he told her. Then he shoved a few sticks of wood into the stove and, with his back to both of them, said, "Go to bed. In morning we talk."

It was only after she was back in bed that Nell realized she hadn't said a word about Louisa. She doubted Peter had. He would probably be fast asleep before Joe was halfway through his supper. Tomorrow, she thought, waiting for sleep to come. Tomorrow would be time enough to get everything sorted out.

8/Suspicions

It was hard to talk to Joe Pennowit. Nell had the feeling that his mind was on something else. Still, he tended Louisa's foot. First he concocted an evil-smelling brew, then he carried Louisa into the kitchen-parlor and made her soak the blue, swollen foot; after that he wrapped it in burdock leaves steeped in hot vinegar. When Louisa flinched, he raised her foot on his fingerless hand and clamped it firmly with the other.

"Better?" he asked.

Louisa sucked in her breath. After a moment she nodded.

"Keep leaves wet," he told Nell. "We eat now."

At breakfast Peter asked him what he had done for food all week.

"Hunted," he said shortly.

"Without a gun?"

"Snares first. Later I have guns."

"How—"

"When you take cows down road, no mention me."

"But the Cartwrights should know they were wrong about you," Peter objected.

Joe shook his head. "Not yet. Jessie first."

"Will you write to her?" Nell asked him.

Joe shook his head. "We go. Show her you are fine."

"Go to Maine?" Nell exclaimed. "But why?"

Joe said, "You make corn bread?"

"Yes. No. I don't know." Why wouldn't he answer her?

"I don't like this tea," Louisa announced after sipping a brew he had made for her out of bits of bark and ground hemlock.

"You'd better drink it, anyway," Peter told her. "It will make you well."

"I want what you're having."

Joe said, "You finish first that tea." He turned to Nell. "Wheat flour with the cornmeal, all right? And that and that." He was showing her the baking powder and ham fat and molasses. "Make big bread for trip. Wash clothes." He indicated the heap of soiled things lying by the door. Then he unwrapped Louisa's foot. The swelling was already down, the angry purple fading and yellowing. "More soak," he ordered.

Louisa groaned, but she obeyed.

"Now," he declared, poised to go out. "Jessie's letter there." He nodded at Nell.

What did he want of her?

Peter pointed to the flatiron on the sideboard. "She left a letter for Gabe just in case he came back first. Grandfather wants you to read it."

Nell saw the letter under the iron. Without touching the paper, she glanced at the first words: "My dearest Gabe, what do you think?" Nell looked from Peter to his grandfather. "But I can't read this." It wasn't like the letter from the Home. "It's private."

"Read," Joe directed.

She shoved the flatiron aside, tearing the paper. "I've spoiled it now."

Joe said, "Writing still there. Read."

Nell brought the torn edges of the paper together. She read of Mrs. Fowler's decision to return to her parents before the weather changed and travel became difficult, a hard decision. It wrenched her heart to think of Gabe returning to an empty house, although Peter might remain.

Mrs. Fowler wrote about how reluctant she had been to believe the Cartwrights' awful suspicions. How could Joe betray her trust and abandon Peter? Nell didn't read that part aloud; she guessed Peter already knew what she was skipping. "The Cartwrights will keep the stock through the winter if Peter decides to leave. They doubt Joe will dare to return, even after he sells the girl. I keep thinking about her. It makes me ill to think what may have become of that poor child." Nell read on silently. "I have to inform the Home without knowing anything at all."

"Read," said Joe.

Nell squinted, as if trying to decipher a word. "'I feel sad to leave our new home. It is hard to leave behind the cradle you made for our child.'" Nell skipped to the end and read the signature, "'Your loving wife, Jessie Macomber Fowler.'"

Joe turned on his heel and strode from the house. Nell appealed to Peter. Mrs. Fowler needed to hear from them at once. Peter didn't seem to know how to answer her. Nodding in agreement, he mumbled something about moving the cows and followed his grandfather outdoors.

It was baffling that neither Peter nor Joe appeared to be in a hurry to set Mrs. Fowler's mind at ease. But Nell didn't voice her concern to Louisa. She just set about bathing her and getting her into clean clothes. Then, after mixing the corn-bread batter and setting it in the oven to bake, Nell went out to find a washtub and to haul water from the spring. Catching sight of Peter and Joe with Seesur, she stopped a moment in the hope that Joe might answer some questions.

Bent over, Seesur's foot gripped between his legs, Joe pushed up with the stump hand while trimming the hoof with the other. Nell couldn't help being fascinated, even though she was sickened by the look of the mutilated hand.

Peter stirred pitch and tar in a pail over a small fire and then held it out to Joe, who smeared the hoof with the sticky black stuff and set the shoe over it. Seesur's shaggy fetlock bounced with every blow of the hammer nailing on the shoe.

"I should stay here," Nell blurted. "With Louisa. You'll go faster that way. You can bring Mrs. Fowler back with you."

Joe glanced up at her before releasing the massive, newly shod foot. "What I say to her, Jessie? You think she believe me now?"

Nell tried again. "We could write a letter. That would be quicker."

"Potatoes," he said to Peter.

"You can help me," Peter told Nell. "I'll give you a sack to fill."

Thinking that she would rather do anything than go back to filling potato sacks, Nell explained that she needed to do the wash first. So Peter helped her haul water and carry the laundry tub out from the sink room so that she wouldn't get the floor all wet.

"Something baking?" he asked.

"Oh!" She ran inside, then had to grab Joe's dirty shirt for a pot holder, to get the corn bread out of the oven. It was only burned around the edges and on top, so she felt she had been spared the shame of complete failure.

"Smells good," Louisa said.

Nell repacked Louisa's foot in the burdock leaves. "By and by, you'll have a taste," Nell promised. "Better get some rest while you can."

Nell did the wash in two batches, first her things and Louisa's, then Peter's and Joe's. But Joe's clothes were so foul, they required extra soaking. Brown clouds swirled up, turning the soft soap the color of red clay. She was still at this job when Peter went by with two cows. He said he would be gone awhile, as it was nearly three miles down to the Cartwrights'. Then he would be back for the sow and the sheep. Nell hoped that while he was there, the Cartwrights would talk some sense into him. The trouble was that if they didn't know about Joe and his plan, they couldn't very well advise Peter to send a letter instead. Wringing out the last of Joe's wash, Nell said, "I guess you'd like to set them straight about your grandfather."

Peter just looked at her.

"I mean, don't you want to tell them *something*?"

"Like what?"

"You know. So they'll be sorry they made Mrs. Fowler think so badly of him."

"And have them come here to see for themselves? You know the first thing they would do about Louisa? Send her back to Mugaleep Mountain."

That silenced Nell. It was just beginning to dawn on her that Peter was uneasy, too.

Every hour or so Nell moved the clothes into another sunny spot so they would dry. She used stones and split firewood to hold them down from the wind. And all afternoon she watched Joe unloading and reloading the wagon with sacks of flour and corn-meal, kegs and boxes, and even a bundle of furs. When Peter returned and told Joe that the Cartwrights had said they would get the rest of the stock later tomorrow, Joe set him to work forking hay onto the rear of the wagon.

"Why do you have to take so much?" Nell asked.

"Get eggs," said Joe.

"But why? I don't know where the eggs are."

"Because we need them," Joe told her, deliberately avoiding her real question. "Look in barn in hay."

Later, when Nell brought all the dry clothes inside, Peter told her to pack them in the cradle along with any winter things from Mrs. Fowler's chest that would fit on top. Just in case, he added, in case she decided to stay on in Pawnook with her folks.

Louisa, hobbling about using a chair in front of her, helped Nell choose what to bring. She picked up a small box made of shells and insisted that Nell include it. Even though it served no winter purpose, Nell gave in and wrapped the box in a shift. She went on packing bedclothes, extra woolen stockings, and wrist warmers.

Louisa collapsed on the bed with another treasure, a candle holder from the nightstand. "This, too," she pleaded.

"No room," Nell said, dragging the cradle to the door.

Peter, coming in, helped her carry it through.

"Matches," Joe called to him. "Tin with matches. Sugar, too."

Together they brought the packed cradle to the wagon. In the last of the light, gunmetal glinted where rifles and a shotgun were lashed to the side. Nell wondered whether Joe expected any more trouble from those robbers, but she knew better than to try to get him to say.

Later, though, when supper was over and all the food packed up, Nell made one more attempt. "If we stay in Maine, all of us, and Mr. Fowler gets back here before we do, he'll think all the bad things the neighbors do. He'll believe them about you."

Joe looked up from the sheepskin he was cutting. "Write it letter, then."

She jumped up, but he nodded her down. "First wax thread." He showed her how to ply two strands, then seal the ply with wax. Peter was punching holes in another piece of sheepskin to tie on under the harness so it wouldn't rub Seesur raw. But Joe was making a boot for Louisa's foot, since she couldn't yet fit in her own shoe.

"Finish one thing," he told Nell, "before you start another."

Sighing, she bent over the strands.

When the boot was done, Louisa beamed at Joe. "It's a—" She broke off, coloring. "I can't remember what they're called. Ladies have them."

"Slipper?" Nell offered.

"That's it. Slipper. I never thought I'd have one."

"Make other next time," Joe responded. Then he turned to Peter, to remind him about extra rope, and went back out to the wagon.

Looking everywhere for writing paper, Nell had to settle on an envelope containing recipes. She struggled to come up with the right, short words to fit. "I am Nell Haskins," she began, "from the Home." She turned to Peter. "How do you spell Pennowit?"

"Just say Joe," Peter told her.

She wrote, "Bad men knocked Joe down and stole the wagon.

He stayed in the woods to find them. I got the horse and wagon away. I got lost. I am sorry I took so long. Please do not blame Joe. He is taking us to Mrs. Fowler to show her he can be trusted. Do not worry about the cradle. He brought it with us. He is doing his best. Your grateful Nell."

She showed the letter to Peter, who mouthed the words as he read them. When he finished, he said, "I was in a Home, too. In New York. They taught us mostly work, not reading and writing. It's the Asylum for Orphan and Destitute Indian Children. It's how I found out I was part Indian."

"Is New York far away?"

"Pretty far. Do you know where Massachusetts is? My father worked in a railroad tunnel that goes under a mountain. One end is in Massachusetts and the other end is in New York. My father was killed in that tunnel."

"What about your mother?"

"She died when my baby brother was born. Then my father got us a new mother. After he was killed, she couldn't keep me anymore, so I was put in the asylum. A long time later Grandfather came for me."

"You must have been so glad."

Peter shrugged. "Not really. I'd never seen him before. He said he was going to teach me his ways so I could be a guide like him. Before he was a guide he was a river driver, but it takes two hands to be one."

Nell didn't have the slightest idea what a river driver was. She said, "It must be hard to get along with only one hand." She tried to imagine what it would be like to go off with a stranger who said he was your grandfather. A question about Indians stealing children nearly tumbled from her lips, but she caught herself in time. If only she could ask the Cartwrights where their suspicions came from.

Peter said, "I help Grandfather. I don't mind. But I can't be like him. I'm going to work on a railroad. That's what I aim to do."

Later, in bed, Nell overheard Peter and Joe in the other room. "What if they come here looking?" Peter blurted. Joe cut in with a sharp warning, and Peter's voice dropped.

He sounded so scared. Was he speaking of the robbers or the Warburtons? Either way, all this haste and secrecy did make a kind of sense to Nell. So did the thorough packing. It was thrifty to fill the wagon with things Mrs. Fowler might want in Maine. Especially the cradle, if she decided to stay on with her parents until the baby was born. Maybe Joe intended to deliver the children and the things and then return with Peter to take care of the farm through the winter. Maybe he looked forward to showing those Cartwright neighbors that the Fowler family could depend on him.

9/The Nowhere Road

I t poured. Nell hoped Joe would change his mind about an
early start. It was a day for staying warm and dry beside the
stove. But when he wrapped Louisa in a rubber blanket and
carried her first to the privy and then to the wagon, Nell gave up
all hope of putting off their trip.

Seesur hung his head against the downpour and did not move.
Nell could see, even at a run, how neatly the rubber cover was
roped over the lumps and bulges. The second rubber blanket
sloped down from the seat and made a kind of tent for the girls. A
moment after Nell crawled under the flap to join Louisa, Peter
thrust a crate of hens in beside her. They were soaked and fussed,
but soon quieted down under the cover.

Hearing pounding, Nell peered out from beneath the rubber
tent. Joe, his hat pulled down in the teeming rain, was nailing battens across the windows. It looked so final. Why was
Joe so sure he wouldn't be returning, with or without Mrs.
Fowler?

The wagon started with a lurch. Louisa twisted around to protect her foot, banged her head against the rubber tent roof, and
released a torrent of water over them. She squealed and grabbed
for the buffalo robe.

"All right down there?" Peter called from the seat.

Trying to scoop some of the puddles over the side, Nell looked
up for a moment. How cold Peter and Joe must be with the rain
pelting them and no protection. "Fine," she called back, and
ducked underneath again. She told Louisa they must be as still as
the hens.

The wagon rattled along the road, everything clanking and

splashing and filling Nell's head with an unending din. She kept hoping that the rain would let up before they reached Woodville. Then she would ask Joe to let her stop at the mill for a moment. She wanted to let the miller and his wife know where they were going. Should she mention Louisa? She felt that she might; then again, there could be trouble. It would be safest to keep Louisa hidden until they were well past Mugaleep Mountain.

On they went, hour after hour, and down came the rain. By the time they crossed the bridge into town, it was raining harder than ever. The few people Nell glimpsed when she raised the flap had their cloaks pulled way up over their bent heads. Nell couldn't expect Joe and Peter, who must be soaked through, to stop just for her.

She watched the town slip past. Here were the houses and shops. There were the railroad tracks. Soon Seesur would bring them to the sawmills and to the road up Mugaleep Mountain.

Not wanting Louisa to realize how close they were to the Warburtons, Nell pulled her head back inside. When she pulled off her shawl, it spattered Louisa and the hens. They all protested, and then Louisa giggled.

"This is like a little house," she confided. "It's fun going like this."

Nell smiled her agreement. The truth was, she felt stifled here. She saw herself and Louisa as baggage, like the captive hens sharing their tiny shelter.

It was nearly dark when the rain let up. Joe stopped to rest the horse and let him drink from a pond beside the road. As soon as Nell got down on the ground, she felt like running and running. But first she had to help Louisa hobble into the woods. By the time they got back to the wagon, the rain had picked up a little and they were both glad to get in under their rubber tent, where they found corn bread, hard-boiled eggs, and apples waiting for them. It was amazing how this cold, private picnic restored

Nell's spirits. The long, dismal day was transformed into an adventure.

"Maybe tomorrow we'll come to a big town and stop and have a hot meal in the railroad depot or an inn."

Louisa, taking alternate bites of corn bread and apple, nodded happily. She seldom thought about the next meal when she had one in front of her.

"We might have a pudding," Nell went on. "And cake."

Louisa grinned and chased crumbs that spilled from her mouth.

While the girls spent the night in their wagon nest, Peter and Joe slept underneath the wagon. In the morning everything dripped. The sky was a sodden blanket, so heavy and wet that Nell wanted to push it away. Seesur, free of shafts and harness, browsed on moss and yellow leaves. His jaws were working all the time, as though he knew the day ahead would be long and hard.

When Nell and Louisa came back from the pond, Joe had a small, smoky fire going and there were singed feathers scattered over the ground. For a while the chicken sizzling over the sputtering flames gave off an acrid smell that took away Nell's appetite. But she shared a mug of tea with Louisa. They took turns scraping up the sticky maple sugar that was left in the tea leaves. After that Nell went running over the spongy ground. By the time the chicken was roasted, Nell was ready for her portion. And then it was time to load up and be on their way.

The hens clucked and grumbled when the wagon started forward. Then they subsided, muttering sullenly among themselves. From time to time one of them stretched and tried to beat its wings. Nell tried not to watch, but every once in a while she found herself staring into the hen's vacant, reddened eye. She wished Joe would hurry up and kill them; she daydreamed about letting them go free.

The road worsened. There were boggy stretches where logs laid crosswise were all that kept the wagon from sinking into the mire.

Twice everyone but Louisa had to get down and gather spruce boughs to spread in a rut.

By evening everyone was as gloomy as the weather. All Nell wanted was to be left alone to rest her shaken body, but Louisa wanted to talk.

"When will we come to that town?"

"What town?"

"The one with the pudding and cake."

"I don't know. Ask Joe, ask Peter."

"Peter, when will we come to the town? Where are we?"

"Nowhere," said Peter, walking away from the wagon, getting out of earshot.

The next day the heavy clouds lifted enough to let some real sunlight through the trees. Nell kept hoping Joe would stop for a rest at one of the small settlements they passed, but he always chose a desolate clearing at the mouth of an old logging road. Every sign of civilization looked inviting to Nell, even a log cabin surrounded by raw stumps.

When they came abreast of a little farm and children ran into the road to stop them, Nell's heart surged with joy. Only the children weren't offering hospitality; they were calling for help. Like starlings, they flew shrilling at Joe. The mare was down with colic; they were sure she would die.

Joe went with them, Nell and Peter following, and Louisa limped slowly after them. The horse lay bloated on her side, her hind legs thrashing in pain. The children's mother sat on an upturned pail, gazing at the death throes.

To Nell's horror, Joe began to beat the mare. He was so calmly brutal as he flogged her that no one said anything, no one tried to interfere. Just as the horse flung her head sideways and struggled to her feet to avoid the blows, Joe grabbed her halter and dragged her out of the barn.

"Get stick," he roared at Peter. "Hit her, hit her."

Peter caught up with them and smacked her on the rump, but she faltered, anyway, and went down on her knees. Joe took the stick from Peter and told him to lead the mare, to keep her moving. Then Joe kept after her, striking her every time she seemed on the verge of collapsing. They went round and round the muddy barnyard like this until finally Joe saw that she could walk along without being flogged.

"Don't let her stop," he ordered, and then he went to search out the cause of the colic.

The woman leaned against the barn door, sagging with relief. "I don't know how we'd get through the winter without her," she said.

Joe reappeared to inform her that her corn was moldy. "Burn him corn," he advised, "or it kill all stock."

The woman shook her head. What was the good of saving the mare if she couldn't feed her? There was no way they could get through the winter without corn. Her men wouldn't be home from logging until spring.

Joe dealt swiftly with the woman's predicament, providing her with a sack of cornmeal in exchange for a sheep. That would give the woman time to seek help from neighbors.

"It's not his cornmeal to give away," Nell whispered to Peter after he had handed the lead rope over to one of the children.

Peter tried to scrape the mud from his shoes and pants. "He's just doing what Gabe Fowler would do."

Joe did more than that. He killed and skinned the sheep and gave a generous portion of the meat to the woman to cook for all of them.

"I don't want to stay here," Louisa whispered.

"We're not. Only for dinner. Try to be nice."

A girl about Nell's size stared at Louisa's sheepskin boot. "Where's the one for the other foot?" she asked Louisa.

Louisa limped closer to Nell and looked at the ground.

"Don't she talk?"

"She's shy with strangers," Nell said.

"Johnny is like that, too. He don't talk. He's our big brother."

"It must be hard having him away till spring."

"He stays longer. Goes on the river with the logs to the mill."

Nell said, "I saw logs on the river back in Woodville."

"Those would be the leftovers," the girl told her. "In the spring when the water's high, there's logs from one end to the other. Our brother Johnny, he can walk clear across on them without sinking. You want to see our puppies?"

Puppies! Nell certainly did, but Louisa wouldn't budge.

"You give your sore foot a rest," Nell told her. "I won't be long." Feeling lighthearted and free, Nell followed the girl into the barn again. The puppies were just big enough to waddle around after their lanky mother, an amiable hound already bored with her offspring. The two girls kneeled in the loose hay while the pups tumbled around them and chewed on their shoes.

Nell lost all track of time. She and the girl talked and played with the pups until one of the other children called them in to the meal. To Nell's annoyance, Louisa was still sitting on the ground where she had left her, rocking slightly and moaning.

"I'm back, Louisa, I'm here," Nell told her. She couldn't help adding, "You could have come, too." As Nell helped Louisa to stand, the girl eyed her warily.

Peter and Joe came in from washing and rubbing down the mare. She was eating hay now. The crisis was over.

The mutton stew with cabbage and carrots and potatoes was enough for many meals to come. The farm children seemed awed by so much meat at once. Peter and Joe and Nell and Louisa helped themselves to huge portions before going on their way. Seesur had just finished the hay put out for him, and was given a drink of water.

The woman and her children lined up along the road to wave the travelers on. Louisa settled back in the wagon nest with obvious relief and didn't even look at the waving children. Nell felt sad to leave them. The girl might have become her friend.

Nell waved as hard as she could and called, "Say good-bye to the puppies. Hug them for me."

The girl squinted up at her but didn't speak. Probably she couldn't hear Nell with the wagon jouncing and rattling and making such a racket.

10/Looking for Tracks

To make up for the hours lost at the little farm, Joe kept going all night. Nell woke once, stiff with cold, and found Louisa rolled inside the buffalo robe. Nell tugged to free a corner of it for herself. She could see Joe's head nodding. Peter, his shoulders blanketed, sat upright, but the reins were slack in his hands. Seesur picked his way over the rough moonlit road.

In the morning, frost was everywhere. Even the rubber blanket was sheathed in ice. Louisa refused to get out of her warm nest until the oatmeal was bubbling in the pot over the fire.

How much longer? Nell wondered. It seemed to her that they were inching through the wilderness with winter nipping at their heels.

Late in the day, Joe pulled up at a fork in the road and stared long and hard. Then he questioned Peter about last night's driving. Sometime during the predawn hours they had taken a wrong turn. Joe pondered some more. Should they go left and try to find the railroad tracks?

"Couldn't we go back instead?" asked Nell. "Then we'd know where we are for sure."

Joe shook his head. "Can't turn him wagon. Road too bad." He decided to head southeast, even though the road seemed to take them through vast reaches of swamp. He had nothing more to say.

Nell wanted to ask him what would happen if they met another wagon. How could they get past each other without going off the log road? But she didn't know how to break into Joe's brooding silence.

Toward sundown he stopped right on the road, unhitched the

horse, and freed him from the harness. Seesur made straight for the water, wallowing in the mud, drinking, and then wallowing some more. When he returned on his own, dark and glistening, Joe led him around to the rear of the wagon.

"What's he doing?" Louisa demanded. "Is he going to beat him because he got all muddy?"

Nell swung around to catch Peter before he went back there, too. "Would your grandfather do that?" she asked.

"Don't be silly," Peter told her. "He only hit the mare to get her up quick, or that would've been the end of her."

Nell couldn't help seeing that beating in her mind, Joe so heartlessly matter-of-fact. "Are you sure?" she asked Peter.

"Of course. Listen, I worked in a mine with pit ponies. That's what happens when they go down with colic."

"I didn't like it," Louisa said. "It was mean."

"He saved that mare, didn't he?" Holding on to the side of the wagon, Peter made his way toward the rear.

Nell climbed down to follow him. It was hard getting around the wagon without slipping off the logs. "Did you really work in a mine?" she asked doubtfully. How many places could he have been in?

Peter paused to answer her. "After Grandfather brought me north. He went to be a guide and had to leave me awhile. That's when he got to know Gabe Fowler."

Nell thought of the mine boys they had seen from the first train, a double line of them blinking in the sunlight. At the sight of their blackened faces Louisa had started to cry. She thought they had been in a fire and were charred.

"Nonsense, it's coal dust," Miss Kingston had snapped. "Just be thankful you'll be working in the healthy country air."

Peter went on around the back of the wagon where Joe had tied the horse. Peter yanked some hay out for him, then dug into a keg and came up with a handful of salt. Seesur kept on licking Peter's fingers long after the salt was gone.

Louisa, who had crawled on top of the load and was looking down on the horse, asked Peter whether Seesur ever bit him. Peter laughed. Not if he held his palm flat, he told her. "Only never do it this way," he warned, sticking his fingers straight up. As soon as Seesur started to nibble at them, he jerked his hand away.

"Was he going to bite them?" Louisa wanted to know.

"Right off." Peter clutched his fingers with his other hand to show her where. "Just like Grandfather."

"Don't tease her," Nell said.

"Did the horse eat his hand?"

Peter shook his head. "Grandfather lost it on the river."

Louisa recoiled in horror. "Lost his hand?"

Peter's gaze slid from Louisa to Nell, who put in quickly, "Not really lost. Peter means there was an accident. Isn't that right?"

Peter nodded. "You talk to her," he said to Nell.

She could see that he'd had enough of Louisa and wanted to get away. But there was nowhere to walk except on the road, and Joe had already disappeared around a bend. Slithering and stumbling, Peter ran to catch up with him.

Nell clambered back onto the wagon. Following Peter's example, she dug around under the rubber blanket until she found the sack of oatmeal Joe had opened that morning. Helping herself to a fistful of oats, she threw it into the chicken crate. The four remaining hens clucked with excitement and gobbled down every single grain.

Later Peter came back for the girls. Joe had a fire going on a kind of island off the road. There was clean water around it and a beaver dam. Peter carried a leg of mutton to roast. Nell and Louisa carried the buffalo robe and a blanket. They gathered around the ruins of a huge stone fireplace, all that was left of a lumber camp that had burned and then been flooded by the dam the beavers had built beyond it. Joe sent Peter back to fetch the chicken crate, and the hens were let out to scratch and forage. They went wild, darting greedily from one rotten log to another.

Dirt flew under them as they hurled themselves on all the bugs and worms they unearthed.

Early in the morning, gunshots woke Nell. She sat bolt upright, shivering, waiting. When she heard nothing more, she snuggled back down close to Louisa and fell asleep again. The next time she awoke, Joe was sitting a short distance from the fire, stretching beaver skins on curved frames made from young saplings. His hands and sleeves and chest were smeared with blood and slime. Nell's stomach tumbled when he reached over to turn a stick with meat smoking on it and offered her a bite.

"What is it?" she asked him.

"Beaver tail. Good."

She shook her head, turning away when he cut a piece for Louisa to try.

Louisa crunched it with relish. Fat dribbled down her chin.

"You're welcome to my share, too," Peter told her.

Louisa took the stick and held it closer to the hot embers.

Joe nodded his approval. "Make good Indian girl someday maybe."

"Fine," Peter told him. "She can have my share of that, too."

As soon as Nell had a chance to speak to Peter alone, she asked him why Joe was taking time to hunt beaver when he had been in such haste before. Peter told her that Joe thought they would be coming to a big town quite soon. He planned to sell all the furs he could. That didn't exactly answer her question, though. There seemed to be no rhyme or reason to the way Joe traveled.

Later, when Peter had brushed the mud out of Seesur's coat and they were packing up to leave, it suddenly occurred to Nell that if Joe sold the skins and had money and there was a railway depot in the big town, she might be able to convince him to send her and Louisa the rest of the way by train. She began to muster arguments: Mrs. Fowler would want them to come the way she did; it was faster than by horse and wagon, so her mind would be set at ease sooner. What else? Nell racked her brains for more ways to persuade him.

They would have to look presentable, too. She made Louisa change her outer clothing, and scrubbed their things in the clear water. Joe flung her his shirt to wash along with them. Recalling the stench and filth the last time, she was afraid she would never get it clean without soap. Holding the garment suspended over the water, she found that she could look at it, handle it, with only a twinge of queasiness. It was different from before. Or was it just that *she* was different?

It wasn't long before the road worsened. Twice the wagon got stuck on rotten logs. By the time Nell helped Joe and Peter get it rolling again, she didn't look much better than she had before the morning's washing. To make matters worse, it began to rain again. Nell and Louisa huddled under their rubber blanket. They saw and heard nothing until suddenly the whine and roar of sawmills cut through the wagon rumble in their ears.

All in an instant the world was restored to them. The road had forked onto a wider one that took them alongside a river. Lifting the rubber flap, Nell caught a glimpse of logs being sluiced through a long chute. Then more buildings blocked her view. Joe was calling to someone, asking about their location. Seesur plodded on.

Nell combed her fingers through her hair and tried to straighten her part. Louisa's curls were a hopeless tangle, but maybe there would be time to dig out the satchel and use the hairbrush. That was the one advantage to having plain, straight hair, thought Nell. It didn't get as mussed as curls.

They were passing a store with a picture of soap in the window. Next came a bakery with golden loaves of bread. Beside it, another store offered DRUGS, HARDWARE, LUMBERMEN'S SUPPLIES. Why wasn't Joe stopping? Was he going to drive straight through when this town might have a railroad depot in addition to all these wonderful shops? "Dry goods," she read out loud. Surely he would think of something he needed to buy. "Fishing tackle. Ammunition." Her voice rose. "Prices moderate."

If Joe heard her, he wasn't enticed. He wouldn't even let Seesur slow down.

"You're letting in the rain," Louisa complained.

Nell pulled her head inside and dropped the flap. Within minutes the town had vanished. She could almost believe she had dreamed it up. When she allowed herself one final glimpse, all she could see was the river. No tracks. No railroad tracks on either side of this miserable road.

11/Across the Border

Toward the end of the afternoon the rain stopped. Now there were cabins and houses and real farms with harvested cornfields and gently rolling pastures. The river had broadened since the last town. It glided over rocks and swept debris into its rushing current with gathering force. Then the road curved away. Gripping the back of the seat behind Peter, Nell stood up as the wagon trundled along. They were descending a long hill, but she caught a glimpse of the river's steep pitch and heard the roar of falls.

"Look!" she shouted into Peter's ear.

Even Joe turned as they came abreast of the churning, crashing river. It sent spray skyward like erupting steam. As the water dropped, so did the road. With a thrill of excitement Nell realized they were coming into a big town, maybe even a city. It spread out before them—streets, mills and factories, wagons and carriages in every direction, and people everywhere on errands postponed by the earlier rain.

The road became the broadway of the town. Joe stopped Seesur across from a three-story hotel with hay wagons lined up in front of it. Now that he was here, Joe seemed in more of a hurry than ever. He hauled out the bundle of furs; Peter untied the new beaver skin from its frame and then called up to Nell to give Seesur a feed of oats in his nose bag.

While Nell scooped oats into the bag, Louisa limped off down the street. Nell wanted to warn her to stay close, but getting the bag on Seesur took all her attention. He kept nudging her so hard that she staggered backward, and then he tossed his head with impatience. An elderly man stepped over to her and slipped the strap behind Seesur's ears.

"Thank you," she said. "I couldn't reach."

"It'll take some growing before you can," he remarked with a smile. "Going far?"

She nodded.

"Well, I hope the horse is sharpshod. There's talk of snow on the way."

Warmed by his friendliness, she asked him if a train stopped here.

Turning to leave, he pointed across the road to the hotel. "There's a stage. They'll tell you the schedule in there."

"But no train at all?" she called after him.

"Not yet," he answered. "It'll be coming."

Coming! If it was expected soon and heading the right way, all she had to do was persuade Joe to send her and Louisa the rest of the way by train.

"Louisa!" she called.

Louisa turned from a window display. "There's raincoats," she shouted. "And rubber boots."

Passersby stared at the big girl with the loud voice and the unruly mop of yellow hair. Best to leave her where she was and go alone to the hotel.

Dodging horses and carriages and scooting past the hay wagons, Nell ran until she reached the imposing pillars on either side of the great door. A sign beside it declared LADIES AND GENTS DINING. There was no reason not to enter the hotel, but she couldn't help feeling unprepared. Inside, everything seemed oversize, the easy chairs and curtains richly colored in brown and gold. Cigar smoke hung in the air. There was a discreet hum of voices all around.

A man stood up behind a tall desk. "I think you want the rear entrance."

Nell's hands flew to her face. She should have taken time to check herself in a store window.

"You can't stop here," the man told her.

"I've come about the train," she said.

"There is no train. Now off you go."

"But I was told—" What exactly had the elderly man said? "Isn't the train coming?"

Another man rose from one of the easy chairs. "Can I help you?" Other people seated around looked up. Nell clutched at her skirt, trying to fold the mud spatters out of sight.

"Please, I was looking for the train that's coming."

The man behind the desk said, "We can't have this here. You're disturbing the guests."

"I'm a guest," said the man who had risen from the chair, "and I am also a railroad man. I believe in treating travelers with courtesy, whatever their age." He turned to Nell. "The railroad is coming in a few years' time. That's what I'm here about. But there is a stage that connects with the New Brunswick Railway. Where do you want to go?"

"To Maine," Nell said, trying not to notice the hotelman's disapproving scowl.

"She doesn't need a stage. She doesn't need a train," he declared curtly. He turned to Nell. "All you have to do is cross the bridge down the road and you'll be there."

"Really? In Maine?"

A few of the people sitting around tittered, but the railroad man quietly asked Nell what part of Maine she wanted. When she told him, he shook his head. He hadn't heard of Pawnook, but then Maine was a big state. There was a stage connection to either the New Brunswick Railway or the European and North American Railway, which would take her all the way to Bangor. It depended where Pawnook was located.

"You want a reservation for Woodstock?" the hotelman called across the lobby. "Or Mattawamkeag?"

Nell had never heard of either place. "I'll have to find out more first," she answered.

The railroad man looked concerned. "Are you by yourself?"

Nell shook her head. Suddenly all she wanted was to be out of there and away from all those watchers. Her face aflame, she mumbled her thanks and made for the door. The railroad man was there ahead of her, opening it, smiling. For an instant she was tempted to blurt out everything to him. But what could he possibly do? She wasn't really lost. Looking outdoors, she saw that Joe had brought Seesur alongside one of the hay wagons. And now he caught sight of her. She couldn't even ask for help.

"Go to Peter," he said as she came up to him. "At grocery store."

Nell ran across to the store, where she found Peter trying to keep Louisa quiet while he finished shopping.

"You take care of this," he told Nell. He dropped some coins into her hand. "I have to pick up a parcel from another shop." He was out the door and down the road before she could ask him what she was supposed to buy. But the saleswoman already knew. Nell had only to wait for the order to be filled.

"Look at the fruit drops," Louisa bellowed. "Here's a barley sugar horse like Seesur."

"Louisa, hush," Nell said, pausing beside the pickle barrel and longing to dip her finger into the brine for one taste.

The saleslady handed her a bulky bundle. "Can you manage this?" she asked. "Maybe your sister can carry the hardtack."

Nell handed over the money. She breathed in the pungent aroma of lemons, the spicy sweetness of iced biscuits. "Yes, thank you," she said.

And then the woman handed her two fruit drops, which Nell couldn't turn down. Louisa held the hardtack so tight, Nell could hear it break. Telling Louisa to thank the woman, Nell hurried her outside.

"But I liked it there," Louisa protested. "Can I have my fruit drop?" She popped it in her mouth and sucked juicily. Nell hurried her along to the wagon and told her to climb up and stay there.

Peter had finished his errand and was helping Joe tuck things away, the rifles and shotguns under the hay now, new supplies protruding.

"Cover well," Joe said. "Big snow coming, I think. Early winter." He went striding off in the dusk.

"Where's he going?" Nell asked Peter, who was stowing salt pork beside what remained of the mutton.

"The blacksmith. We'll pick him up on the road."

Louisa shouted down to her, "Look what's here!"

Nell couldn't see up over the load.

"Stockings," Louisa crowed. "Mufflers and rubber boots and gloves."

"Don't touch," Nell called to her as a matter of course. "They're not yours."

Peter snubbed the rope down. "Yes they are. Grandfather told me to get them for you both."

"For me?" shrieked Louisa. "Mine?"

"Come on," Peter told Nell. "Time to go."

But Nell stood there puzzling over all Joe's arrangements. What was he up to? What was he thinking of?

"Come on," Peter said again.

Nell walked slowly around to the front of the wagon. She needed to speak to Peter before they picked Joe up at the blacksmith's. "Why?" she asked him. "Why winter things," she went on, taking all the time she could, "and all these provisions, when Maine is on the other side of the river?"

Peter whipped around. "Where did you find that out?"

Nell tried to make him meet her eyes. "I asked. I've been asking."

But he refused to face her. "You shouldn't. You'll just get us in trouble."

"Why?" she demanded. "What kind of trouble? There's a secret, isn't there? Something you're not saying. Why?"

Peter gave an exasperated sigh. "Just get up here. Grandfather's waiting. Whatever you do, don't talk . . . don't talk to people." He lifted the reins.

Hiking up her skirt, Nell pulled herself onto the seat.

"Not here," he said.

"Tell me," she insisted.

"Get in back." He slapped the reins, the wagon lurched, and Nell went sprawling. Grabbing hold of her, he shoved her toward the back. "What's got into you?" he demanded. "One dummy is enough on this wagon."

"Stop it," she hissed. "Don't talk like that."

They passed the stores. One shopkeeper was closing his door for the night. And there ahead in the road stood Joe with another parcel. Nell slid back into the nest full of winter treasures. Joe tried to unload his parcel, but it rolled out from his fingerless hand. Nell blocked it from falling. It was very heavy.

"Good," he said with a nod. "Stow later. We go on now."

They came to a big stone bridge. Nell could just make out the date, 1860, carved on a block in the facing bulwark, but it was too dark to see the water tumbling below.

Louisa said she had to get down and go into the woods.

"Not yet," Joe told her. "No woods here."

How did he know what was here and what was not?

"Customs House," he said to Peter. "You stay." He was on the ground and striding into the darkness toward someone with a lantern.

The lantern approached. "Evening," said a voice. "Going on through tonight?" The speaker was at the rear of the wagon. "No furs?" he said. He poked and prodded; the hens cackled and then fell silent. "And this? A cradle? That's fine, that's enough."

In a few minutes they were continuing on. When they stopped again, it was to let Louisa go off the side of the road. Nell took advantage of the stop, too. Joe acted edgy until they were under way again. Nell had no idea what was wrong with him. They had crossed from Canada into the United States of America, but nothing seemed any different. The cold descended; the moon rose, blurred but bright. Louisa nestled in among the store-bought treasures and fell asleep.

But Nell stayed awake. She didn't want to miss the next town they came to. Now that they were in Maine, she felt sure that anyone she asked would be able to tell her how far they were from Pawnook.

After a long, silent stretch she heard Peter say to Joe, "No one knows. You can tell no one knows."

"Maybe," Joe answered, his voice low but natural. Nell was sure they believed her to be fast asleep. "Maybe they catch up, maybe let law catch up."

"They're robbers, Grandfather. No one pays attention to men like them."

Nell had to clench her jaws to keep her teeth from chattering. She had a feeling there was more to what they were saying than she heard.

"We shouldn't leave this road," Peter insisted. "The sooner we get to Pawnook, the sooner Jessie Fowler will be able to help."

"No help," Joe said. "Help for white man maybe, not for Indian."

"What if there's a big snow? What if it's a blizzard?"

"Snow come, snow go. Moon of Rattling Leaves still to come. We get better chance in woods."

Nell tried to unlock her arms. She would have to wait for the wagon to reach a rough place before she dared snuggle down beside Louisa and pull the robe over her head. She didn't want them to know that she was awake and listening.

When the plunging and jostling began, she welcomed it because it allowed her to move without being heard. The trouble was, it kept on like that, rough and noisy. Nell drew her knees up tight and waited for the steady motion to resume. Any moment now the road would become smooth again. It was only a matter of time, that was all. As long as she was all covered up and could see nothing, it was possible to go on believing this was simply a bad stretch they were on, not the woods.

12/Seeing Things

Waking under the robe and realizing that she wasn't being jounced around anymore, Nell's first thought was that they were back on good road. Relief warmed her. Even now they must be coming into a town, because she could hear thuds—someone chopping wood. Groping for the edge of the buffalo robe, the cold truth dawned on her. The wagon wasn't just smooth, it was still.

She pushed aside the robe. There was Peter dragging a huge hemlock bough toward the wagon. He beckoned to her. Still dull with sleep, Nell looked everywhere for the road. They were surrounded by trees and boulders and, just ahead, a rocky stream.

"What are we doing here?" she asked Peter.

"Making a bridge."

Louisa poked her head up and called, "Where are we?"

Nell shifted the question to Peter, who replied, "Maine."

"Why are we in the woods?"

"Snow coming," said Joe as he shook a cramp from his good hand. "Road gets slick. Wheels slip."

While Seesur pawed and ate his way through a heap of hay, the girls joined Peter, helping him to haul hemlock and spruce boughs to the stream. Louisa, wearing new rubber overshoes and a woolen muffler, stumbled a good deal and had to stop often to rest her foot. "When will we eat?" she asked. No one answered.

Peter showed Nell how to lay the boughs and branches so they overlapped. That meant she had to step into the stream. She gasped as the icy water filled her shoes. Her stockings and skirt were wicks drawing the wetness up and up.

"We have enough now," Louisa finally declared.

Joe came over to test the evergreen bridge and shook his head. "More," he said.

Nell tried to warm her raw fingers under her chin. Nothing helped, though, because as soon as she grabbed the next prickly branch and set it in the stream, her fingers stung and ached all over again.

She decided to go straight to Joe and protest. He had no business taking them off into the woods like this.

Joe shoved the end of a small fir tree at her. He nodded her away.

"I want to talk to you," she said.

"Later," he told her. "Work now, so we go far before snow stop us." Shouldering the ax, he moved off toward another fir.

Nell yanked at the little tree to get it started. Suddenly Peter appeared in front of her and reached for the tree. "Here," he said, "it's too heavy for you."

"I can do it," she snapped, venting her frustration on him. She gave a tremendous tug and tipped right over on her back.

Peter looked down at her as tears splashed her frozen cheeks. "Are you hurt?" he demanded.

"No."

"Why are you crying?"

"I'm not." She rubbed her eyes and nose. "We shouldn't be here. We shouldn't be doing this."

"We'll be all right," Peter said. "Grandfather will take care of you."

"I don't want him to. I want to take the train." She gazed up into the treetops at the dingy-looking sky. Something like a scrap of ash wafted downward and landed on her forehead. Another followed, feather-light and aimless. She sat up. She couldn't understand why Peter didn't agree with her about being here when last night he had pleaded with his grandfather to stay on the road. What had Joe said to make Peter change his mind? If only she had stayed awake to hear them. "And now it's snowing," she said. She couldn't help making it sound like Peter's fault.

"Nothing to speak of," he said, helping her up. "It's not even sticking to anything." But his face was drawn with worry as he picked up Nell's tree and dragged it to the stream.

It took most of the morning to make the bridge dense enough for the horse and wagon. Seesur seemed to sense its weakness, his great hoofs striking out wide to seek more solid footing as he scrambled across.

Nell thought they would stop now and light a fire and eat, but Joe kept them pushing on. The snow stayed light, but the way was crowded with blow-downs, and Joe and Peter had to stay ahead to clear a path. No one spoke, except Louisa, who recited complaints about her foot and her empty stomach in a low singsong as she trudged with Nell behind the wagon. When Joe stopped to let Seesur drink from a pond, he boosted Louisa onto the wagon and distributed hardtack to each of them.

Nell, her legs chapped and wet, had lost all sense of time. She crammed the dry, flat bread into her mouth, and then had to chew and chew to make it go down. By the time she realized she needed a drink, they were on their way again, the pond behind them.

The snow got heavier as the day wore on, the walking harder. As the land rose, Nell tried to hold on to the rear of the wagon for support, but it moved so jerkily that it threw her off balance. She leaned into the climb, her legs pumping painfully, while the snow surrounded her with unnatural brightness. With each step she saw less. A wind came up, driving the flakes right into her face. Poor Seesur, she thought. How could he forge ahead, snow-blind and exhausted?

Then she walked into the wagon. At first she couldn't tell what had happened. Louisa let out a wail from above. Joe shouted to Peter. Stumbling, Nell made her way around to the front to find Seesur on his knees.

They had to unhitch Seesur to get him up. Then for a while

they struggled to free the wagon, which was hung up on a snow-covered outcrop. Finally Joe gave up and went to look for a sheltered spot to set up camp for the night. They would need full daylight to jack up the wagon without doing any damage to it.

Joe found an even bigger outcrop of ledge that made a wall against the rising wind. They went back and forth between the wagon and the sheltered place, carrying food for themselves and Seesur. They gathered deadwood for a fire and snow for the kettle. Nell was so tired, she could hardly eat. But she gulped down the hot, sweetened tea, held out her cup for more, and then watched greedily as Joe cut off a small chunk of maple sugar and plopped it in.

The snow held back the dark and sealed them in a strange twilight. Joe brought the girls to the wagon and made sure they were settled under the buffalo robe and the rubber blanket. Then he carried another blanket back to the sheltering ledge for himself and Peter. Nell was asleep before he walked away.

Nell dreamed they were left alone. She knew the dream so well that it would have been reassuring if it hadn't struck such terror in her. All the Home children dreamed of being abandoned, especially the shipwrecked ones. They were supposed to overcome those fancies with faith and reason. The thing to do was to walk right out of the dream into the everyday world.

The buffalo robe resisted. It didn't want her to thrust it aside. "Cover up," Louisa grumbled. "It's cold."

There. The everyday world was Louisa, complaining and sleepy.

Nell pushed back the weight, the darkness, and came into a ghostly light that was neither night nor day. Rubbing wet snow from her eyes, she gazed all around until she thought she spied the iron pot hanging from the stick across two forked branches. Only no fire crackled under it. The black pot swung slowly in a sudden gust and lost its shape, its density, its blackness.

Nell kept looking. No fire, no Seesur, no sign of Joe and Peter. Had the nightmare of her life come true? She groped for the overshoes. Then she wrapped her head and shoulders in the shawl and slid down. She sank into waist-high drifts. With her back against the wagon, she faced toward the outcrop. She could remember going in that direction. It must be there, along the ridge, out of sight.

Head down, hands clutching the shawl, she slogged through snow of varying depths. She couldn't be sure where she stepped, so she let the wind guide her, veering off it just enough to keep her eyes open. Floundering, she fell twice. The second time she turned a little more. She felt stronger with the wind at her back. Only it was useless peering through the whitened trees. She could scarcely tell up from down.

There was no way to guess how far she had come. She knew she would have to face the wind again if she didn't want to miss the ledge. Not yet, though. She was afraid of having to shut her eyes.

She hitched up her skirt because it was binding her legs, and then she couldn't even feel her legs. Maybe she should go back to the wagon and start over. But she hated to lose the ground she had already made. She would go on a little longer this way.

Plunging from a solid foothold to a dip in the ground under the snow, she pitched forward. Winded, she took a moment to get her breath back and pulled herself to her knees. Here she was in a kind of nest. It felt good to be still. Her ears still pounded, though, the sound of surf inside her head. She had to fight off the sensation of waves rocking her. She was more afraid of that motion than of wind and snow.

She struggled to her feet. She tried to brush the snow caked on her skirt and shawl, but she only spread it more. Through a white blur she saw something immense and dark looming just ahead. Seesur! That meant the fireplace was nearby, too.

He stared through the snow at her. Probably she looked different to him. Everything looked different in a blizzard, especially Seesur himself. His face was distorted, bloated. "Seesur, good boy," she tried to say to him, but her lips were too stiff to form the words. She would have to go to him, and then he would lead her to safety.

She walked through waves of snow and slammed into something—a branch, perhaps—that struck her over the eyes. She cried out, not in pain but in surprise. When she opened her eyes, Seesur was gone. "Seesur!" She gulped for breath as panic gripped her by the throat. "Seesur, Seesur!"

She was still gasping his name when a mittened hand grabbed her shoulder and yanked her around. Her own screams went on ringing in her ears. Yet somehow, outside of her head, she could hear Peter's hoarse shouts informing his grandfather that Nell was found.

"If you ever do this again . . ." he rasped, trying to haul her by the sleeve.

Do what? she wondered. Why was he trying to pull her sleeve off? She felt herself lifted and hoisted facedown over someone's shoulder. Her head began to pound, her eyes to throb.

The fire sputtered and smoked in front of the shelter. Joe rolled her in his blanket and called orders to Peter, who was to bring Louisa and clothes and oats for the horse. Nell tried to tell Joe that Seesur had run off, but she had such an attack of shivering that she couldn't utter a word.

Later, with dry clothes on and hot cornmeal mush inside her, Nell found her voice again.

"Next time," Joe said to her, "you stay put or wear hobbles like him horse."

"Seesur isn't hobbled," she answered. "He ran away from me."

Joe shook his head. "Not him. He never run."

"He did. I saw him."

Joe sat back on his heels. "People see things in snow, see stories." He held a wad of snow on the lump over her right eye. She could tell from the look on his face that the subject was closed.

13/Story by the Fire

L ate in the day the snow tapered off. After Peter led Seesur back and forth to make a trail between the shelter and the wagon, it seemed no distance at all. Nell felt ashamed of having strayed so far and gotten lost.

To prove herself capable, she tried to help the others extend the shelter with spruce boughs. Joe propped trunks and limbs to form sides, then covered them and roofed them over with the dense, springy evergreens. But Nell didn't do very well. Her head throbbed whenever she leaned over; her eyes teared from the brightness of the snow.

She decided to cook a stew for their supper and asked Louisa to fetch potatoes and carrots. But Louisa forgot the carrots, so Nell went herself, squinting to avoid the low, dull light that intensified the whiteness all around. Just before she reached the wagon, something enormous on the far side wheeled, and then stopped to gaze at her. Was it a trick of the light or her smarting eyes that made the animal seem so huge? She tried to open her eyes all the way. Bigger than Seesur, she thought, bigger than a cow.

She stood absolutely still, amazed but not frightened, perhaps because the wagon was between them. What was this creature with the big ears and the long, mournful face descending to a loose, bulbous muzzle? It had the look of an animal invented by someone with too much imagination. Only it was real; Nell hadn't dreamed it up.

She wasn't aware of moving, but she must have, because it suddenly went striding off on its long, awkward-looking legs. Despite its clumsy appearance, it fled swiftly through the trees, becoming in an instant a large brown blur.

She waited a moment, just in case the animal changed its mind and returned. But it was gone now. To Nell's dismay, it had left plenty of evidence of its visit, having raided the potato sack that Louisa had forgotten to cover. Nell gathered up half-eaten potatoes strewn over the snow and on the hay. She took them back to put in the stew, along with carrots and onions, and decided not to say a word about the raid to Joe and Peter. They would only blame Louisa and be hard on her. The only way to teach Louisa to be careful was to remind her just before her next errand, when there was some chance that she wouldn't forget.

But Nell was curious about the great brown animal. When they were sitting around the fire that night, she asked Joe what kind of big animals lived in these woods.

"One time," Joe answered, "all animals big."

"She doesn't mean your old stories," Peter declared curtly.

Joe peered through the smoke and beyond. "Of Old Time," he continued, ignoring Peter, "of Old Time Glooskeb make all animals very big. Glooskeb was first here in land of sunrise. Made squirrel big as wolf. Then squirrel say he scratch down trees on Glooskeb's people."

"Where did his people come from?" Peter interrupted. "You said Glooskeb came first."

Joe nodded. "Took bow and arrow, shot at basket-tree."

"A tree with baskets?" Peter laughed.

"Tree that baskets made from. Glooskeb shot at tree called ash tree. People came out of bark. When squirrel say he kill the People, Glooskeb took him squirrel in hands and smoothed him small like all you see now in woods. So with every animal."

"Watch out," Peter warned Nell. "It can take all night getting through that story. When Grandfather says every animal, he means all the way down to the ants."

Joe fell silent then. Nell gave up for the moment. She would think of another way to find out about the animal that took their potatoes.

"I liked it," Louisa murmured sleepily. "I liked that story."

"All those Glooskeb stories," Peter informed her, "they're heathen."

"How do you know that?" Nell asked him.

"In the asylum they told us to forget the old Indian stories. Of course," he added, "I had no idea what they were talking about, since I'd never heard any. Learn Scripture, they said, and forget the rest."

Joe shook his head. He spoke into the fire. "People must remember."

Peter shrugged. In an undertone he said to Nell, "I'm sure he was taught the same as me. He had a priest for a teacher. He told me that once."

They were far from the question Nell had asked. She lay down next to Louisa, taking care to turn on her left side and covering her right eye with her hand to keep anything from touching it.

In the morning Joe and Peter woke her as they came puffing and grunting to the fire. Off before dawn to hunt rabbits, they had come upon an injured caribou. Peter was exultant because Joe had let him shoot it, but bringing it back was another matter, especially without Seesur to haul it for them. They worked all morning, cutting strips of meat to smoke over the fire and roasting one huge haunch.

Louisa was fascinated. "Glooskeb forgot to make it small," she remarked to Joe.

Pausing over the carcass, his bloodied knife upraised, he said, "Bigger ones than this. Many days eating here, though."

"Why bother with it?" Nell asked. "Seesur can't carry all that extra meat. It'll just slow us down."

"We can't leave yet," Peter told her. "Too much snow."

"I wish we'd stayed on the road," she murmured. "I wish we'd go. If we're already in Maine, how much farther can it be?"

"I don't know," Peter said. "You'll have to ask Grandfather."

Nell looked over at Joe. He was kneeling, pressing part of the caribou carcass against his chest with his fingerless hand and thrusting his knife upward to slice the meat from the bone.

She walked closer. He didn't look up. She crouched down and asked him how long it would take them to reach Pawnook.

He went right on with his butchering. "One time," he said, his words broken by the strokes of the knife, "all woods and rivers belong to People. No border then. Tall pine trees in woods, rivers running this way, that way. No one stop them rivers, no one take all trees. People free like rivers, fast in spring down to sea, slower going back to woods to hunt in winter."

"But what about now?" Nell persisted. "We're not going to the sea and this isn't the spring. When will we get to Pawnook?"

"Good luck," Peter muttered as he heaved himself up and walked off.

Nell waited. Joe shook his head.

"Different now," he continued. "Trees gone, rivers turned, game killed. Winter come too soon. Different—"

Peter came crashing into their midst. "Moose!" he shouted. "At the wagon. A moose!" He grabbed one of the rifles. "Can I have the first shot?"

"Put down gun," Joe said. He stood up. "We look." Gesturing to Peter and the girls to stay behind him, Joe led them along the path. Nell couldn't help thinking she was about to see the strange brown animal that was neither horse nor cow. Only how could it be a moose? Didn't moose have great, spreading antlers?

The moose, or whatever it was, was gone. Peter was bitterly disappointed.

Joe studied the hoofprints and pronounced them moose. "Young," he added, yanking the rubber blanket back over the salt. "Maybe like to come with us."

"If only I'd had the rifle," Peter said.

"You killed caribou. We have meat."

They walked back to the shelter, Peter dejected, Joe thoughtful. Seesur was hobbled and let go to browse where he could. The girls spent the rest of the day hauling and stacking wood. They needed to keep the fire smoking to cure all the caribou meat.

The night was bitterly cold. Joe sent Peter to bring hay for the horse and told him to scatter a little near the wagon. Peter argued that they were running low on horse feed. Joe insisted.

The next morning the moose had returned and eaten the scattered hay.

"Now we'll *have* to kill him," Peter declared.

"Now leave salt," Joe countered. "When hay gone, moose show horse other food in woods. You see."

"Is a moose like a cow?" Louisa asked anxiously. "Will I have to take care of it?"

Joe smiled. "Moose take care of moose. And maybe horse. Then, when we need," he finished, thumping his mutilated hand on his stomach, "moose take care of us, too."

During the day the air warmed, melting snow on boulders and branches. The woods teemed with life now, birds dropping from treetops to the bloodstained snow, crows strident and watchful, squirrels spiraling up trunks and chittering wildly. Joe began to clean the caribou skin; the smoking of the meat went on.

That night Peter decided to sleep on the wagon. He wanted to see the moose when it came for salt. Louisa shivered at the thought of him all alone and exposed to the biting wind. Wrapping herself in the buffalo robe, she huddled deep in the shelter.

But Nell wasn't ready to go to sleep. She crept closer to the fire, where Joe scraped and rubbed the flesh side of the hide. It kept slipping out of his grasp, so she took hold of it for him, trying to roll the hair side over the slimy part to avoid gripping the raw skin. The smell of the hide and the scrapings that clung to Joe's clothes combined with the smoking meat and reminded her of the stench from the things she had washed at the Fowler farm. She turned her face away, but it didn't help.

A tiny ripple whipped an overhead branch. Joe's steady rhythm kept Nell from starting. Then Joe held still to listen, but there wasn't another sound from above.

"Owl," Joe said softly. "Smell him caribou."

How could he tell? Nell hadn't heard its wings at all. She gazed down at the skin between them. Joe moved and partly turned it. She could see by firelight the deep brown shaded to cream. "Beautiful," she murmured.

"Yes, fine thing," Joe answered. Leaning across it, he reached out with his stump and touched Nell's head. She froze. "Warm hat and shoes. You see." He went back to his scraping.

She squeezed her eyes tight shut and drew a long breath. "I heard you the night we came here. Talking to Peter." When he made no response, she opened her eyes. Louisa, sleeping in the darkness of the shelter, seemed far away. There was only Nell here with Joe, the caribou skin between them. "You left the road. You were running away. Why are you afraid? What more can they do to you?"

Joe took a long time to answer. "They knock me down, you know. Hurt me. First thing, nothing. I go nowhere, two day, maybe three. Then . . . then I hunt. Hunt them men, you understand."

Nell nodded. "But how did you know where to look for them?"

"I listen. One whole day only that, listen."

"You heard them?"

Joe shook his head. "Not them, not yet. Hear crows, hear animals come to fireplace." He paused. There was only the slick whisper of the knife. "Then," he went on, "I find them. Only horse and wagon gone, you gone. I wait. When they sleep, I take all guns and hide them. And I go back to them. To him, to make him, this man I know long time ago, make him say what they done with you."

Nell could picture the sleeping men, just as she had seen them that first night. She couldn't picture Joe there with them.

Joe held his mutilated hand up to her face. She couldn't turn away. It was too late to close her eyes to what he was showing her.

"This hand hold him." In a gesture so quick that Nell flinched, Joe dropped the hide and swept the crooked knife back toward himself. "Wake him, say where child now? This hand hold him man. Speak softly, say where child be?"

Nell couldn't take her eyes from the poised knife.

"Come from sleep, that man. Come yelling, fighting." The knife wobbled in Joe's fingered hand and then drove at the hand stump that seemed to hold someone up against him.

Nell held her breath. Slowly Joe's arms went limp. He wiped the knife on his knee and went back to scraping the caribou skin.

"Then what happened?" she whispered.

"Happened?" Joe shook his head. "What can I do? I run."

"But was he all right?" He was bleeding. She knew now that the blood she had washed came from that man.

"I kill him."

"Are you sure? How can you be sure if you ran away?"

"I know," he answered. "I always think about killing him since long time. So," he finished, all tension gone from his voice, "now you see."

Speechless, she nodded. There was nothing more to ask, to say. She knew that he would go on scraping the hide until the job was done. By then it would be the next day or the day after that, and nothing would be changed for him. She didn't even think about herself or Louisa. She didn't want to think—or to sleep, either. So she sat there and kept on helping to hold the caribou skin tight, her mind frozen, waiting for the night to be over.

14/Louisa's Find

J ust before dawn something got at the chickens. Peter had set the crate out of the way of the wagon. He didn't see the animal that killed two of the hens. As soon as Joe heard the squawking, he picked up a rifle and ran, but the killer escaped.

There were tracks, though. Joe followed them past sunrise, and then returned to set a trap farther off from camp. He used one of the dead hens for bait and hung the other right next to the shelter to keep it from the crows.

Nell couldn't bear having it so close, but she said nothing. She felt cut off by what she had learned; she felt helpless and baffled. Crawling inside the shelter, she retreated from the day's activities. She pretended to sleep.

Meanwhile Joe fashioned moccasins for her and for Louisa, who was overjoyed with hers and brought Nell's to her. The inside had warming caribou hair.

"You have to wear them now," Louisa said, "and then they'll get to be the shape of your feet. Try them, Nell. Your toes won't be cold anymore." Nell didn't want to touch them. Finally Louisa gave up and went off on her own.

Later in the day she came back full of excitement. She had found something. She wanted Nell to come with her right away.

Grudgingly Nell emerged into the afternoon sunshine and let Louisa drag her along the ridge. More snow had melted. It was easier to walk without tripping over obstacles hidden by the snow. Roots and stumps, blow-downs, and rocks all revealed their shapes beneath the snow cover. Red squirrels flashed in and out among the trees and paused to rail at Louisa as she stooped at the base of an oak.

Nell peered down. Louisa seemed to have unearthed a cache of acorns or nuts. Nell was about to suggest that she leave what was there for the squirrels, who no doubt had put them there, when she saw Louisa pointing at something else protruding beside a twisted root, something that looked like the hand of a large doll.

"Can I touch it?" Louisa asked. "Can I take it?"

Nell squatted down for a closer look. A hand bent back at the wrist, the fingers curved but not closed in a fist. "Of course you can," Nell said. "It won't hurt you."

Louisa pulled. For a moment nothing happened. Nell thought it must be stuck in the frozen ground. Then suddenly it came away in Louisa's hand. Beyond the wrist of the hand-shape was a blade; the wooden hand was a knife hilt. It was the oddest-looking knife Nell had ever seen, but it was bent in the same way as Joe's.

Louisa couldn't stop babbling over her good fortune. "This is my best day. New shoes and now a knife of my own. I can keep it, can't I?"

"Keep what?" Peter crossed in front of their path and stopped. "What's all the fuss about?"

Louisa showed him the knife.

Peter reached for it, but Louisa snatched it away from him.

"I just want to look," he protested.

Louisa extended it toward him but still held on to it.

"It's rusty," he said. "Where did you find it?"

Louisa gestured along the ridge.

"Can I have it? Girls don't use knives."

"Yes, we do," Nell shot back. "We have lots of things to do with knives. Louisa, don't give it to him."

Louisa clutched it with both hands and drew it to her chest.

"You'll just hurt yourself," Peter told her. "Anyway, it'll probably bust the first time you use it."

Louisa broke from the path. Still clutching the knife, she waddled through the deeper snow and ran, elbows flapping, past the shelter and on toward the wagon.

Peter watched her go. "Why does she run that way?" he asked Nell. "She talks funny, too. What's the matter with her?"

Nell thought if she could explain about Louisa, he might be kinder to her. She tried to begin with the shipwreck; only she had to start with her own story and how she had been rescued along with other children. "The people on the island spoke another language. They had a few other children from an earlier shipwreck. Louisa was one of those. She hardly spoke at all then. Mostly she would whisper a little. We kept trying to find out her name. All we could hear was 'Slue'—something like that. So we called her Sue Lou. When we came to Canada, they gave her a new name in the Home, a proper name, Louisa."

Peter was frowning, shaking his head. "Hasn't she had enough time now?" he asked. "Shouldn't she be . . . more like other people?"

"I don't know," Nell answered. "How can you ever really know what other people are like?" She was thinking about Joe. She was thinking that Peter must be aware of everything Joe had told her last night. Still, he went on from day to day knowing his grandfather was a murderer and not telling. Nell would never look at Joe again without seeing his hand thrusting the knife down and back. If only he hadn't killed the man because of her. She felt tainted by that connection. It brought back the stench of the blood she had washed from Joe's clothes. She felt trapped and helpless.

She realized she hadn't really answered Peter's question about Louisa. She simply told him, "Louisa has feelings like other people. She minds when you make fun of her."

They parted then, Peter taking off for the wagon, Nell returning to the shelter. She didn't realize that Joe and Peter were jacking up the wagon and getting it ready for travel until everyone gathered at the fire after dark.

They didn't leave the next day. Joe had trapped and killed two raccoons, but he knew from the tracks he found that a fisher cat was after the hens, and he was determined to catch it.

Peter tried to remind him about the urgency of their errand. "Jessie Fowler still thinks you stole Nell and Seesur and the wagon."

"One day more," Joe replied, "snow down. Black cat pelt bring more money than three beaver. Very hard to find him black cat."

Louisa was perfectly happy where she was. She didn't mind the delay. But she did notice Nell's sullen mood.

"Are you worried because the oats are gone?" she asked.

Nell shook her head. For that matter, they were almost out of hay, too. If they were nearly at Pawnook, it didn't matter. If they still had a long way to go . . . what then? Nell wondered. What should she do? What could she do? Speaking mostly to herself, she said, "We might come to a town."

"In the woods?" Louisa sounded surprised.

"We might come to a road first, and then a town. And if that happens, Louisa, we might have to stop and find someone to stay with for a while."

"And not go to Mrs. Fowler?"

"Not this way. Not with Joe."

"Why not?" Louisa's voice rose. "Why can't we go with Joe?"

"Ssh," Nell cautioned. "You have to keep your voice down. This is a secret. You can't tell anyone. I don't know if we'll get a chance to stop. We have to be ready, that's all. It's not good for us to be here like this."

But Louisa was too stirred up to keep her voice down. What wasn't good about having caribou moccasins and enough to eat? And how did Nell know that someone in a town might not be like the Warburtons?

"They won't be," Nell promised. "If they let us stay, it will be someone good and kind."

"Joe is good and kind," Louisa retorted. "I'm staying with him."

Nell had to get away by herself. Telling Louisa that she was going to take Seesur browsing in a fresh place, she untied him and led him downhill in search of the black alder that he liked to eat. She thought about telling Louisa the truth about Joe. But it was impossible to guess what effect it would have on her. The worst thing would be if Louisa asked Joe a lot of questions and made him angry. She wouldn't understand that he could be dangerous.

Seesur scooped the snow aside and chomped on the reindeer moss that grew in thick green patches between the trees. Nell dropped the lead rope and let it trail in the snow. Every once in a while Seesur picked up his head and stared off into the distance, his great brown eyes intense and dark, his furry ears pricked forward. She noticed that his coat had grown shaggier since she'd first seen him.

When she thought he was straying too far, she hurried after him. Stooping to retrieve the rope, she noticed that Seesur was covering his own tracks. Brought up short, he stopped and gazed intently beyond her. Nell swung around in time to glimpse the brown hindquarters of a moose. At least that's what she thought it must be. Only where were its antlers? She saw its large, erect ears distinctly until it slipped into the dark shade. Then it turned for an instant and stepped into the light. A moose without horns, then; high-shouldered, big-nosed, long-legged.

Seesur gave a soft, throaty call. The moose lifted its heavy head, showing the skin flap that dangled from its lower jaw.

Nell wasn't exactly afraid, but she moved a little closer to Seesur. The moose lowered its head and vanished among the trees.

Once the moose was gone, Nell led Seesur back. Joe glanced up from his work as she tied Seesur to the tree. For one instant it crossed her mind that he had been worried. Did he think she would have taken the horse and run away?

"Seesur was hungry," she said, pointing to the tree that was stripped of its bark. "I took him to eat, but I don't think he got enough."

Joe dropped his knife and raised his hands over the fire, then dipped them twice, as though scooping up smoke. "This much cornmeal in feedbag," he allowed. Then he added, his voice guarded, "You miss dinner. Bring sugar, too." The fingers of his good hand were still cupped to show her the measure of cornmeal for Seesur. She tried hard not to look at the other hand.

But after she took care of Seesur she had to bring Joe the large chunk of maple sugar and wait while he hacked off the amount he wanted. He pressed the block of sugar against his chest with the mutilated hand. Even turning from him, she knew the gesture. She could see the knife come down, dig in.

She took her bowl of sweetened cornmeal porridge into the shelter. She was glad that he hadn't offered her meat. She would have turned it down. Did Joe sense that? Nell couldn't tell. It seemed to her that they were like the moose and the horse now, alert to each other but keeping a certain distance, too.

15/The Other Side of the Rain

Joe got his fisher cat that night, and the next morning Seesur was harnessed and hitched to the wagon. Even with the smoked meat added, the load was lighter than when they were stopped by the snowstorm. The hay was down, the oats gone. Still, Joe insisted that everyone walk to make the pulling easier. They were all kept busy dragging aside branches and blowdowns. It was slow going and hard. No one wasted breath talking.

When darkness fell, everyone except Nell ate cold meat. She was too tired to bother with food. She climbed up onto the wagon and pulled the buffalo robe over herself. She was asleep before Louisa joined her.

When it was time to hitch up Seesur at dawn, the hoofprints of the moose were intermingled with the horse's.

"Good," Joe declared. "Help him horse feed. We give him moose salt tonight."

On they went, this day warmer than the day before, with more slush to get through. Sometimes when a wheel bogged down, Seesur just quit until they all pushed and lifted to free the wheel. Nell could see brown water oozing up and filling the hole it left.

After one more day like this, it began to rain. They kept on until the rain washed away the last of the snow and the ground became impassable. Using the wagon for shelter, Joe cut bark in great sheaths from yellow birch and attached them to one side of the wagon. The rubber blanket was kept in place to protect the cornmeal and the cradle. The birch bark became a roof and wall to keep the rain off the travelers, but they weren't able to build a fire near the wagon, so there was no fire at all. Since the smoked caribou was turning slimy, Joe and Peter took rifles and went off in the rain to hunt whatever they could find.

Louisa, the buffalo robe pulled up to her chin, gazed almost vacantly into the dismal, gray woods. "It's nice here," she murmured.

Nell couldn't conceal an impatient sigh.

"You want to hold my knife?"

Nell shook her head. "I want to be dry. I want to be home."

"Home," Louisa echoed dreamily.

Nell glanced at her, wondering what kind of home she had in mind.

"Maybe it's just on the other side of the rain," Louisa said.

"It isn't. There's just more trees. Trees and trees and trees."

"What if there's a big house? There might be one, anyway. What do you call it, with tall things and lots of rooms?"

"A palace?"

"That's right. There's a palace on the other side of the rain, only you can't see it because the trees are in the way. Think what's inside it."

Nell relented. Soon they were making up a story about a palace in the woods. Louisa gave it things she especially liked the sound of, like a room with ladies' furnishings and a barbershop.

"In a palace?" Nell couldn't help laughing.

Louisa laughed, too. "Part of the time it's a greengrocer and a bakery, but you don't have to pay."

"That's right," Nell agreed, "because it's magic. The whole palace is magic. Sometimes it isn't even there, it's invisible."

"Only we can see it, can't we?" Louisa threw the robe off and sat up. "Say we can see it, Nell."

"I meant that. We can, but other people can't. It's like a secret that's only for us. You understand about secrets, Louisa."

Louisa nodded. Reaching for the robe, she sank back. "And bright lamps," she said. "Lots of lights."

"Lots of light," Nell agreed. "I think I'd like to look at your knife, after all."

"It's in your satchel. That's a good hiding place, isn't it?"

Nell said it certainly was. But later, when she dug down to get it, at the last moment she couldn't bring herself to touch it. She could see that Louisa had cleaned the blade, but it was still encrusted. She had wiped the hand-hilt, too, though the carved wood was pitted and stained. Nell knew it had nothing to do with Joe's stump, but it gave her the same kind of feeling. So she stuffed her clothes back on top and tucked the satchel away again.

Joe and Peter returned with muskrats, but they had no fire to cook them on. They ate cornmeal in rainwater and some maple sugar, and then Joe skinned the muskrats to add to his collection of pelts.

Sometime during the night Seesur broke free from his tether and disappeared. Peter was afraid he was gone for good, but Joe was pleased. He could tell from the tracks just where the moose and horse had come together.

"Moose show him horse alder swamp, willow. You see."

Just about the time the rain let up, Seesur came striding into sight, the moose not far behind. Peter wanted to run to Seesur and hobble or tie him. Nell had the same impulse. What if Seesur changed his mind? What if the moose took off and Seesur followed him?

But Joe gestured them to be still. Seesur walked up to the wagon and nosed at the rubber blanket. Quietly, smoothly, Joe moved toward him. Pausing to give him a brief rub under the long black forelock, Joe rummaged one-handed under the cover and brought out a handful of cornmeal, which he spread over the rubber. Then he stepped back out of the way.

Seesur went to work with his tongue. The moose came forward, eyed the people, and then moved in beside the horse. Seesur laid his ears back, swished his tail, and tried to jostle the moose. Then he went on with his licking, and the moose did, too.

"I've seen him before," Nell whispered. "I didn't know he was a moose. I thought they had horns."

"Not if it's a cow," Peter answered, keeping his voice low.

Louisa drew back. "You promised no cow."

The moose flattened his ears and snorted, sending up a yellow dust cloud.

"Be still," Peter told her. "You scared him. Her. It's not a cow, it's a cow moose."

"Not cow," Joe told him. "Young bull, maybe three, maybe four year." Bringing his hands to his head on either side, he described a width. "Maybe that much horn. Moose sometimes shed horns early winter."

"Ugly," Louisa pronounced, staring at the moose's bulbous nose.

The moose turned his sad, amber eyes on her before moving on to nibble the birch-bark canopy. Joe quietly sent him away with a wave of his hand. After retreating a few steps, the moose pushed aside the leaf mold in the wheel tracks and pulled up stalky roots from the softened ground. Seesur pushed up against him, snatching roots that dangled from the moose's mouth. The moose just dug for more. Gradually he moved farther off. They could hear him tramping through undergrowth, snapping branches, coughing once or twice, as if he were waiting for the horse to follow.

Louisa wanted to know how big the big moose had been in the old time before Glooskeb made him smaller. Joe said in Old Time moose's antlers spread wider than the branches on the tallest tree.

"This moose is as tall as plenty of trees," Louisa pointed out. "Maybe Glooskeb forgot to make it small."

"He's not much bigger than Seesur," Nell said, trying to reassure Louisa.

"Seesur is careful not to step on us," Louisa countered.

"That true," Joe told her. "Keep away from moose. Not used to people, not yet. Now we make fire for dinner."

It took a long time to get a fire started; everything was

drenched and wouldn't burn. Joe nursed along a small, smoky blaze, but it didn't produce enough heat for cooking until dark. By now everyone was keenly interested in hot food. Only Joe remained patient. The fire would take its own time.

Louisa continued to brood about the moose. "I don't think Glooskeb made him small enough," she said to Joe.

A log broke and tumbled from the flames. Kicking it back, Joe said, "In Old Time all animals and People have just one speech."

Nell saw Peter hunch his shoulders, as if to ward off the coming story. She said quickly, "Couldn't we put potatoes around the fire now?"

Peter sent her a grateful glance. Joe nodded and told her to try the potatoes, although he didn't think there were enough embers. The fireplace was only a few yards from the wagon shelter, so she had the potatoes out in no time. Joe laid them inside the circle of stones. He placed another scroll of birch bark on the flame and then added more twigs. The fire spat and smoked and labored on.

"Glooskeb made all the living things just right," Joe said. "Taught the People about hunting, about singing. All could understand. But no one had ears for the rules Glooskeb gave them."

"Why didn't they?" Louisa asked him.

"That is the way of People and animals. This I myself know. Glooskeb tired of bad way. Called them to big feast beside lake."

"A feast for the animals, too?"

"For all. Oats for horse, lily stems for moose, fish for black cat, berries for bear. Everything right like that. Then Glooskeb gets into canoe, paddles away. When he is gone, all them still hear him sing. Then singing goes, too, bit by bit. No sound anymore."

There was a stillness all around the fire, its weak flame like the beating wing of a dying moth.

"No sound," Joe repeated.

Nell found herself leaning toward him to catch his words. Even Peter was attentive, rapt.

"All animals and People trapped in silence, understanding gone.

Each one speaks different way, goes different way, into woods, into lakes, into rivers. Into sky." He turned the potatoes and fed the little flame.

Nell said, "But the moose and Seesur seem to understand each other. And Seesur understands us."

Joe spoke from the depths of his being. "Not in words. Words died with Glooskeb's song. Words won't come until Glooskeb come again. That why things go wrong between People, between animals, between all things. Ever since that time Kweemo—loon—looks for Glooskeb, wailing, calling him home."

Peter sighed. Then he spoke. "The reason things go wrong is that we're sinners."

"That is so," Joe agreed. "Story from Old Time not so different from story priests tell."

"If it's not so different, why do they tell us the old ways are bad?"

"They want our People to be like theirs."

"That's progress," Peter said to him.

Joe regarded him with a steady look. Then he placed his stump hand on Louisa's head. "Lose song, then you forget. You, too, trapped in silence."

Nell was stunned. Joe was saying something important about Louisa. How did he know that she was cut off from her own past and from almost everyone around her? Nell searched his face. In repose it seemed to her ageless and tender. Could a man who spoke and looked this way commit a brutal crime? His voice came into her head: *I always think about killing him.* Nell clutched her ears, but she couldn't block what was already inside. His words, like his deed, were a part of her.

Louisa spoke dreamily. "I like the time before Glooskeb went away."

Peter snickered. "Not me. I like new times. I'm glad of railroad trains and steamships and rubber blankets and canned food. When are we going to eat?"

"Try muskrat now." Joe got up. "Maybe get it roasting."

"I like those things, too," Louisa told Peter. "I had canned peaches once. They tasted good."

Peter swung on Nell. "You see? She doesn't even know what the story was about."

Nell kept still. She refused to get into an argument with Peter just because they were all hungry and tired of the rain. At least Joe's story distracted them for a while.

Much later, when they were feasting on potatoes and muskrat, Joe mentioned that since they had to wait for the ground to harden before going on, he was thinking of buying some hay and other supplies.

For a moment Nell thought he had lost his mind. Peter's jaw dropped. Even Louisa stopped sucking her greasy fingers and gaped at Joe.

"You're planning to buy hay?" Peter asked. "Where?"

"Lumber camp. Not far, I think. See trees new-cut—one, maybe two, years."

"You think you can find it?"

Joe spit a bone into the fire and nodded.

"Will they sell hay?"

Joe nodded again. "For cornmeal, maybe. For furs, guns. You bring enough, you see, you and Nell. Bring money, too."

"You're going to send us to a lumber camp?" Peter exclaimed.

Nell's mind raced. She realized she was about to be presented with the kind of opportunity she had tried to prepare Louisa for. They could go with Peter, and when he was ready to return to Joe, they would stay at the camp instead. Of course, they would work for their food and shelter. They would cook and wash and feed the horses and oxen until they could be sent on their way in safety.

"Lumber camp," she murmured, feeling a kind of astonished hope. Louisa had been right, after all. There was something wonderful out there on the other side of the rain.

16/Shifting Over

The freeze came unevenly, with bitter nights and dull windless days. Gradually the ground hardened, although some especially warm days split the frost crust and left sharp, treacherous rifts below the leaf mold. Joe spent this waiting time hunting. He moved their camp down to a large pond with a beaver lodge at one end and an island half a mile out in it. But he took only two beavers. The rest must remain, he said, to replenish the colony. The reason Joe chose to build a new shelter beside the pond was to keep track of the moose.

And the horse. Because once the move was accomplished and the shelter well packed with spruce boughs, Seesur was allowed to wander with the moose, wading into deep water for the plants still green there and full of nourishment. Every day the moose followed Seesur back to camp for salt or a cornmeal treat. Now Joe could walk around the two animals, stroking the horse first, then the moose, which always ceased tonguing the salt or meal to roll his eye watchfully. Then one day when the moose dropped his head to the salt, Joe tied a rope around his neck and left it on with the end dangling. The moose tried to shake off the rope; Seesur finished the salt.

The next day Joe took hold of the rope. The moose strained away from him for a moment and then pressed hard against Seesur to get at the salt. Joe ran his stump hand over the moose's head and under his jaw. Then he turned to the task of making a rawhide halter. The moose would have to be restrained when Peter and Nell drove Seesur to the lumber camp. If he followed, he would most certainly be shot.

Peter watched Joe cutting caribou hide. Every three strips had to be braided to make the halter strong.

"Why not just hobble him?" Peter suggested.

Joe tied three strips to a wheel spoke so he could tug them tight. "Hobble make him thrash," he answered. "Break leg or worse."

"Then we should shoot him now and trade the meat for hay."

Joe struggled one-handed, the strips slippery in his fingers. "Thought about that," he said. "We might need him moose later."

"Later!" Nell burst out. "Why can't we just go and get there?"

"Hold this," Joe instructed. "Pull. And listen. When ice thick, strong, we go cross pond, downriver, next pond."

Nell hated the way the rawhide oozed in her hands. "Why don't we go around the pond?"

"Pull," he told her.

"I am. It feels like worms."

"Pond and next pond and river all together, long way. Peter finish braid here. Nell make nose bag for him moose. Like this." He showed her how to fold the bark and to stitch it, using long root fibers for thread. "Big for big nose."

Nell liked this work better. The bark smelled wonderful. It was almost pleasant sitting there at the edge of the pond with the feeble sun reflecting back on her. Her fingers were actually warm. The clothes she had washed were drying on branches.

Joe pointed to a tree swimming toward the huge mound of trunks and limbs he called the beaver lodge. Not a tree, he explained softly. The beaver was preparing for freeze, too. Sure enough, while they watched the tree advance toward the mound, the dark, blunt head of the beaver broke the surface of the water. Then down it went, tree and all.

"What happened?" Louisa asked, alarmed. "Did it drown?"

"Go under lodge. Store him tree for ice time. Then beaver have food underneath ice." Joe took the nose bag from Nell and nodded his approval. "Now write," he told her. "Scratch with this." He handed her another section of birch bark and a horseshoe nail. "Write 'sleigh runners.'"

"You're going to leave Mrs. Fowler's wagon there?" Peter was aghast.

Nell wrote S-L-A-Y. It didn't look right.

Joe said, "Shift to runners. Make wagon bobsleigh. Then we go where wheels get stuck."

Nell crossed out S-L-A-Y and scratched instead, R-U-N-N-E-R-S. That looked fine. "What next?" she asked.

"Hay. Maybe oats, too." He went on down a list of supplies.

"Louisa needs to come with us to the lumber camp," Nell said.

Joe shook his head. "Two go, two stay."

"She gets upset when she's left behind."

Joe turned away and started to haul things out of the wagon. Peter went to help him, but Nell stayed apart from them, trying to figure out a way to get Joe to change his mind about Louisa.

That evening Joe kept aloof, too. He left the fire to sit alone at the edge of the pond. The sky was strangely light, but no moon showed—nor cloud, either. Suddenly Louisa came crying toward the shelter. "Fire, fire!" she yelled.

Peter jumped up. "Where?"

"The pond. It's burning!"

Peter looked, and then he laughed. "It's a reflection, dummy. It's not in the water, it's in the sky."

"You mean, the sky is on fire?" Louisa's finger bit into Nell's arm.

"It's the northern lights. It's nothing bad. Look, Louisa, Grandfather's watching them. He isn't afraid."

Louisa, still cowering, glanced at Joe, who sat motionless, his face tipped skyward. Nell looked up, too, and saw the pulsing green-and-blue waves take on a reddish cast and spread like a stain to the farthest reaches of the sky. Clutching herself, Nell shivered. The sky shivered, too.

Louisa let go of Nell's arm and walked over to Joe. Then she sat down beside him. Nell expected Joe to turn his back on Louisa or to get up and stalk off. But he did neither.

Louisa studied him a moment, then drew her knees up, wrapping her arms around them in a perfect imitation of Joe.

Tense with cold, Nell crawled beneath the buffalo robe. But she couldn't get warm. She wondered how long Louisa would go on sitting there under that seething sky.

When Joe woke Nell, he wouldn't let her wake Louisa. Seesur was already harnessed and hitched. The moose, haltered, was roped to Seesur's tree. The nose bag hung so loose on him that he had to fold his gawky forelegs and kneel to rest it on the ground to lick the cornmeal at the bottom of it.

Joe hurried Nell and Peter onto the wagon and slapped Seesur's rump to start them off. Nell twisted around. If only Louisa would spring up now and howl for Nell. But there wasn't a sound from the shelter. Joe stood beside the moose, his good hand on the rope; he had to dodge the moose's foreleg as it struck out at him.

He has us all, thought Nell. The moose, Louisa and me, even Peter. He has us on his tough rope, yanking us any way he wants.

"How can you tell where to go?" she asked Peter.

"Grandfather marked it."

"All the way? He's already been there?"

"This part we cleared together. Farther on, Grandfather went alone; he left signs on trees. After that he says it's a regular logging road."

Thinking she would have to pay careful attention so that she could find her way later on with Louisa, she asked Peter how long it was supposed to take. Peter shrugged. Grandfather had told him he should be at the lumber camp by midday.

"If Louisa does act bad," Nell asked him, "do you think your grandfather will lose his temper with her?"

Peter gave her a surprised look. "Have you ever seen him lose his temper?"

She shook her head. How could Peter pretend he didn't know what Joe had done? She said, "Louisa can make an awfully big fuss. That's what happened in the first family that took us. Everything was fine until the spring when I started school. It wasn't for long, but Louisa doesn't understand about time. She thought I was going to be away every day forever. Mrs. Satterlee said she was impossible. That's why we were sent back to the Home."

"Couldn't they have kept just you?" he asked.

Nell nodded. "They wanted to. They tried to. I would have been happy there. I did all the cleaning and the washing. It was a lot, because it was a doctor's office as well as a home. But it wasn't bad work. On Sunday afternoons they let me take a book from the shelf. I used to read it aloud to Louisa." How she had missed the books when she was back at the Home waiting to be placed again. There, all the stories were short and packed with moral lessons, nothing like the thick volumes of adventure and history at the Satterlees'. "I had to stay with Louisa," Nell tried to explain. "We're almost-sisters."

"Did you have any real sisters or brothers?"

Nell nodded. She told what little she knew about her brother in England, that he had left her because he had no way to keep her, that he had visited her once just before she was sent on the ship to America. Much later those memories began to come and go like half-forgotten dreams, until nothing remained but a longing she couldn't define. After she and the other shipwrecked children were taken from the island, she learned that her brother had returned for her, only to be informed that she had been lost at sea. No one knew his name or where he went after that. Nell liked to imagine that one day they would find each other and he would tell her all about their family.

Peter listened to her without interrupting, without questions. It felt good. When she spoke about her brother, she could almost recall his voice, though he remained faceless to her, like someone seen in a dense fog.

"What about your brother?" she asked Peter.

"He died when he was born. When my mother died."

"So there's only you?"

"And Grandfather," he said. He pointed to a short stick wedged under a strip of bark, cut and raised from the trunk of a tree. "That's one of his signs. We're making good time, I think."

Nell pulled the blanket tight over her shoulders. Even with the late-morning sun filtering down through the green-black fretwork of spruce, she ached with cold. She wished she could trust Peter with her plan to escape with Louisa to the lumber camp. At times like this, he was so easy to talk to. But as long as he kept from her what he knew about Joe, she had to be careful.

Suddenly the woods echoed with a tremendous thud. Distant crows sounded an alarm. Pulling Seesur up, Peter strained to hear more. With the creak and rattle of the wagon silenced, Nell imagined ax blows, voices. Peter shook his head. But just then Seesur raised his muzzle and gave a volley of shrill neighs that rang through the woods.

Peter said, "He knows there are horses."

Heartened, they went on. A pond glinted on their left, a great body of water with long stacked logs on its banks. Seesur was trotting now in springy strides on an open logging road. His neighs were answered by horses they could not see.

When they came into a clearing and saw smoke and the low roof of a building, Peter said quickly, "Remember, we have to make them trade us fair."

Nell supposed he was telling her to let him do the talking, but as soon as she saw a man in a red jacket coming toward them, she threw off the blanket and practically fell from the wagon in her haste to meet him.

"Whereabouts are you from?" he asked. "Didn't know there were any farms close by."

She looked up into the creased face, almost hidden by reddish-gray whiskers. Were his eyes kind? Would he be her friend? "We're not from around here," she answered. "We're travelers."

"Just the two of you?" he exclaimed. "Pretty far off the road, aren't you?"

Nell shot a look at Peter, who was just now joining them. He gave his first name and Nell's, and said the rest of their family was back at their camp.

Telling them to call him Cookee, the man led them into the low building, a kitchen full of stoves and pots and pans and the most delicious smells imaginable. He sat them down on a bench, then set before them plates with pork and beans and fresh, hot bread. Peter tried to explain his errand with his mouth full. Cookee just nodded and promised to speak to the boss when he brought the noontime meal out to the men. Meanwhile Peter and Nell could feed and water the horse, warm up some more, and help themselves to the apple pie over on the crate.

After they helped him carry out kettles and pans of food to a low, ox-drawn sledge, they went back to the kitchen and ate until they felt stuffed. Then, while Peter attended to Seesur, Nell explored the camp. First she peeked inside the sleeping house, a long log building with a dirt floor and stacked wooden bunks that looked like stalls in a barn. At the far end, clothes hung every which way from lines strung up around a huge stove. One whiff inside was all Nell needed to turn away from the door. The stable, which she came to next, was roofed with spruce and turf and had an earthen bank for one wall. It was dark and smelly, too, but better than the bunkhouse.

She found Peter stooped inside the doorway of a root cellar of enormous proportions. It reeked of onions and turnips and earth, but it held the tang of winter apples, too.

"Oh," she breathed, "they have so much."

"That we do," spoke a voice behind her.

Wheeling, they faced Cookee and a shorter man in a fur hat.

"Who sent you?" he demanded. His tone told them he was the boss.

"We're supposed to see if you have runners that could—"

"Cookee told me what you came for. I want to know who's in charge."

"My grandfather," Peter replied.

"Why didn't he come?"

"He's hunting. He's paying our way selling skins."

Nell suppressed a gasp. Peter had managed to duck the question without really lying. She supposed that the boss was uneasy about dealing with children.

"What else besides runners and hay?" asked the boss noncommittally.

"I have a list," Nell said. "Mostly food."

"Show Cookee," he said. "You"—he nodded to Peter—"come and look at what we have. I need to see the wagon, and I want to go through the pelts."

Nell brought out the scrap of birch bark to go over with Cookee.

"How much tea does your grandfather need?" he asked her.

Nell had no idea. She was puzzling over whether to say that she was not Peter's sister, not Joe's granddaughter, when she realized that Cookee had just asked her grandfather's name, and out it came.

"Joe Pennowit!" Cookee exclaimed. "The Indian? Now isn't that a wonder!"

"You know about him?" She could hardly believe her luck. If word had traveled this far about the killing, then she could stay here, after all. The boss would send men after Joe, and they would bring Louisa back with them. "You know?" she cried.

"Of course I do," Cookee answered with a grin. "Boss was just talking about him the other night, telling some of the young fellers. Your grandfather's famous!"

Bewildered, Nell just stood there with the list in her hand, waiting for him to say more.

"Boss!" Cookee shouted. "You'll never guess. Their grandfather is Joe Pennowit, of all people."

Boss looked up from the wagon. So did Peter. Nell's heart sank. It had gone all wrong, and now Peter would be furious with her for revealing Joe's name. But how could he blame her if he refused to tell her why she shouldn't have mentioned it?

They all came together at the wagon, the two men speaking at once, Peter glaring at Nell, and Nell trying to take in everything they were saying.

"My own cousin, you know," Boss was bragging, "all the way to the Connecticut River that time with Joe. They say it was the longest drive ever. Too bad Joe didn't come here himself. I'd be proud to meet him." Boss stopped short. "That must mean it was your father lost down Deadman's Pitch—Joe's son, Tomah."

Peter explained that Joe's daughter was his mother.

"That means Tomah was her brother, your uncle. I suppose you know that your grandfather saved the man that started that trouble."

"He doesn't talk much about that time," Peter mumbled evasively.

"Can't blame him. A bad, bad time. Took his son and took his hand, too. Finished him for a river man." Boss fingered the furs. "So these come from Joe Pennowit. I had no idea he was around these parts. Well, I'll be glad to help him any way I can. Let's see what runners we have that'll fit your wagon." He led Peter off.

"We'll start packing," Cookee told Nell with a smile, "but I doubt we can load up before dark. It'll take a bit of doing, shifting the wagon bed over from the wheels. We'll want it empty for that. I expect your grandfather knows you can't leave before morning on the early frost. Will he be worrying?"

Trying to keep pace with Cookee as he headed for the cellar, Nell shook her head. She was wondering how she would ever convince him and Boss that she needed to be rescued from Joe. If Peter knew what Joe had done and was willing to protect him, how would Cookee and Boss look at the killing? Maybe murder was less than a crime, less than a sin, when the person who committed it was some kind of hero. How could she explain her dread? All she understood was that she had to get away from Joe Pennowit, get away from everything that reminded her of what he had done for her sake.

17/Riches

I t felt different on the bobsleigh, sounded different, too—quieter. Seesur, seen from lower down, looked as if he, too, had been transformed overnight. He could easily be one of the massive logging horses that Nell had glimpsed coming into camp at dusk. Cookee had whisked her into the kitchen when the men returned. He insisted that she stay there until morning. After that she could only guess what the camp was like, full of men and beasts. She had fallen asleep, her head thick with the voices and clatter, and then had awakened much later, feeling too warm, unaccustomed to the heat of the stove.

Now she missed it. The air felt damp and raw. Nothing could keep it from drilling into her body, not even the extra blanket over her shawl.

A mournful wail, hollow and piercing, sounded across the pond. It made Nell think of the creature Joe had named who went on calling Glooskeb through all time. Or was it one of the People who called him? Her teeth began to chatter.

"You'd better eat something," Peter told her. "It'll warm you up."

She reached for the bundle on the seat between them. Unwrapping it, she found roast potatoes, cheese, and half a pie. There was also a small, separate package wrapped in paper.

They ate in silence, relishing every mouthful. Finally Nell unwrapped the small parcel. Chocolate! She inhaled the rich, sweet aroma. "I suppose we ought to save it?" she said uncertainly.

Peter gazed down at it. "Cookee must have meant us to have it or he would have put it in back with everything else. He doesn't know about Louisa."

Nell nodded. "We'll taste it, and then put the rest away." She broke a piece off the slab and handed it over. Breaking off another bit, she tried to leave it on her tongue to melt. But she couldn't help herself. She swallowed it down.

Together she and Peter stared at the remaining chocolate. Then she wrapped it up and tucked it under the seat. The first rays of sun drew frost from the earth in swaths of mist. Nell's eyes burned from the dazzling vapor where webs like spun glass spanned the naked branches and snagged on the spidery tips of poplar and birch.

Peter broke the silence as the bobs ran smoothly on the bed of crusted needles and leaves. "You know, I've never seen Louisa use that knife she found."

Nell shut her eyes against the glare. Her head pounded.

"I was thinking, since you're almost sisters, thinking if you asked her to give it to me, don't you think she would?"

Nell shrugged. She didn't want to talk about Louisa's knife.

"If Grandfather finds out she has it, he won't let her keep it."

"Why not?" Nell murmured.

"Knives are for hunters," Peter said.

And also for murderers, Nell felt like adding. She didn't speak.

"What if I told him she had it?"

"What if I told him," Nell shot back, "that Cookee and Boss know he's in these woods."

"You can't tell him that," Peter cried. "Anyway, it's your fault they know."

"Peter," Nell said, "why does it matter so much? I mean, I know it does, but you haven't told me why."

"It doesn't." But he stumbled over his own answer. "I can't explain."

"Try," she pleaded. "Remember, you warned me about talking to people before, too. In that town with the waterfall. Only it didn't make trouble there, and it didn't make trouble here, either. They were nice to us because of Joe."

Looking straight ahead, Peter blurted, "There may still be trouble. It has to do with those robbers. He . . . was in a fight with one of them. All right? Do you believe me now? Will you promise not to say anything about this to Grandfather?"

Nell nodded. Her head throbbed; her back felt bruised. She had a feeling that if she kept at Peter now, she might goad him into telling the whole truth. Then she, too, could let down her guard. It would be such a relief. She hated being wary and clever.

Just then something crashed through the woods. Seesur stopped short. Nell and Peter could hear branches breaking, and pounding hoofs. Seesur uttered a low greeting as the moose came rushing toward them at his swift, side-rocking gait. He overshot, circled around behind the wagon, and charged up to Seesur. His frayed rope dangled from the rawhide halter.

"Something's happened," Peter said. He clucked to get Seesur started, but the moose stood in his way. Peter looked all around, and then overhead. "It's close to midday. We must be almost there."

His uncertainty alarmed Nell. "Don't you recognize where we are?"

"I guess so. Maybe. It's different coming from this direction." He slapped the reins.

The moose lumbered ahead of them, then came galloping back in another crazy circle. He coughed and snorted, and then he ran full tilt at a tree, hitting it with his head again and again. When he stopped, there were beads of blood between his ears and on his short, bristly mane.

Nell and Peter exchanged a look. Neither of them knew what to make of this strange behavior. But now they could see more blood on the moose's flank. What had he been doing to himself? Why?

"Do you think he hurt Louisa?" Nell asked Peter.

"Grandfather wouldn't let him. He'd shoot him first." Peter hurried Seesur along. Soon Nell could see their pond through the trees. The first thing that caught her eye when they drove into their campground was the tree where the moose had been tied. The earth around it was all torn up; the other end of the rope was still tied around the trunk. Next she saw the baggage they had all helped to unload from the wagon two days before. The cradle was perched on top of everything to keep it dry. It looked so ordinary there and, at the same time, so out of place.

Peter was staring toward the pond, where Louisa and Joe looked up at their coming, though both remained on their knees, poised over something large and black and furry.

"Nell!" Louisa called. "Come and see our bear! Come see!"

Peter opened his mouth, then shut it again. He jumped down from the seat and walked over to look. Nell followed.

Joe said, "Did you get everything?" He peered up at the bobsleigh. "Hay, too? Food?"

"You shot a bear without me?" Peter's voice cracked.

"Yes," Louisa told him excitedly, "and I fished, and we ate the fish last night. I caught them."

"You told me," Peter said to his grandfather, "that we wouldn't find any bear this late. You said they all den up by now."

Joe nodded. "Probably this one turned out by some other bear. Act pretty mad, mad enough to go after moose."

"They were all mixed up together," Louisa chimed in. "Joe thinks the bear could tell that the moose couldn't get away. You should have seen the moose kick with all his feet. He even kicked Joe. Joe says that bear made the moose go wild and crazy."

"Had to cut moose free," Joe went on, "before shoot bear."

They all gazed down at the bear, where it lay stretched in readiness for Joe's knife. Nell turned away.

"Big fire," Joe called after her. "Bear-steak dinner, and then we smoke rest of meat."

Louisa joined her, leaving Peter to help his grandfather with the bear. Together the girls unhitched Seesur and dragged the harness off. Louisa chattered about the fishing and the bear as they gathered wood. They had to go some distance for it, and then hauled it bumpily back to the fireplace. Several times Nell staggered and had to sit still for a moment. Her ears rang and her eyes teared and her head felt as though it had ballooned into something enormous and fragile.

She summoned all her strength to inform Louisa that by this time tomorrow they probably would be at the lumber camp.

"I don't think so," Louisa responded. "Joe says as soon as the ice gets really hard, we're going that way." She pointed out over the pond.

Nell rested against a tree. "Not you and me, though."

Louisa frowned. "Joe didn't say he was sending us somewhere else."

"We're not being sent anywhere," Nell told her. "We're escaping."

Louisa snapped a stick in two and lowered her head.

"We'll be . . . warm where we're going, Louisa. We'll have real bread and apple pie. Wait till I show you what we brought for you. Come to the wagon."

But Louisa was so full of resistance that Nell had to persuade her to taste the chocolate. Then, as soon as she ate it, she was won over.

"Only it's a secret," Nell reminded her. "You mustn't tell."

"All right," Louisa agreed happily. "Who mustn't I tell?"

Nell nodded toward the shore. "Them."

"Peter doesn't know?"

"He's not coming with us. And Joe doesn't want to go there."

Louisa ran her tongue over her lips. "It's just for a little while, isn't it?"

"For a while," Nell agreed cautiously.

But much later, after everyone but Nell had gorged on bear steak and Louisa had soiled herself and her clothes, she seemed to have forgotten Nell's plan for them.

"You can't walk into the lumber camp like that," Nell whispered. "Go and wash."

Louisa looked down at her front. She rubbed the heel of her greasy palm on her skirt.

"Don't," Nell snapped.

"That's what Joe does." Louisa pointed across the fireplace at Joe, who leaned back. Stretching, he held the knife aloft. In the firelight, the upraised blade glistened.

Nell got up to take Louisa by the arm, but Louisa shook her off. Then, sullenly, she allowed Nell to lead her to the water's edge.

"They'll sleep well tonight," Nell whispered. "We'll leave before morning."

"Why didn't you eat anything?" Louisa wanted to know.

"Louisa, after you wash, put on your clean shift and blouse and give those things a good scrubbing."

"It's too cold. There's no room around the fire for drying."

"Just bundle up your wet things. You can dry them at a stove tomorrow." Nell groped through the darkness, in search of her satchel. She realized she would have to move the buffalo robe away from the shelter and the fire, away from Peter and Joe, who were already wrapping themselves in their blankets for the night.

When Louisa trudged back with her roll of sodden clothing, she stood around aimlessly for a moment, then sat down beside Joe.

"Over here," Nell called, a sharpness in her voice.

Louisa came all hangdog. "You're being so mean," she said as she crawled under the robe.

"I'm sorry. I'm just nervous."

Louisa sat bolt upright. "My knife!"

"It's all right. I have my satchel."

Louisa sank down. "This was my best day," she breathed drowsily.

Nell snuggled down beside her. She was afraid of dozing. But sleep dragged her into the darkness.

She awoke with a start when Joe rekindled the fire. She knew she had to stay awake now. As soon as he fell asleep again, it would be a good time to get away. Aching with tension, she rolled onto her back. Finally she was able to see the outline of the tree-tops. If only her hand didn't shake so as she gripped Louisa's shoulder.

"Louisa, time to go." Nell drew back the robe.

"Cold," Louisa mumbled.

"Ssh. You can wear my shawl."

But when Nell started off, Louisa just stood where she was, her teeth chattering. Nell retraced her steps. "Hurry," she whispered.

"We should say good-bye."

The words echoed in Nell's head: *Good-bye, good-bye.* "We didn't say good-bye to the Warburtons."

Louisa whimpered, "I don't want to."

"Anything wrong?" came Peter's sleepy voice.

Nell's heart sank. "No, nothing," she answered.

Dropping to her knees, Louisa drew up the buffalo robe. Nell bent down to explain to her how important it was to leave now, but she couldn't remember why it mattered so much.

Propping herself on her elbow, Louisa raised up the robe for Nell to crawl in beside her.

Shivering, Nell looked through the trees. The metallic glint of dawn was already showing on the pond. She knew she was defeated, at least for now.

"You're so cold," murmured Louisa, on the edge of sleep.

Cold? Nell wasn't really sure how she felt anymore. It was as if she had been running for miles. Her face and back were clammy. It was very strange. She couldn't even catch her breath.

18/Wind-Blower

Nell slept and woke and slept again, always in the green dimness of the shelter. Sometimes she managed to throw off the buffalo robe, but never for long. She was aware of hands covering her, turning her, prying her mouth open. There were even moments when she could feel the bluntness of one of those hands under her chin. Swallowing cut off her air. Gasping, she tried to heave herself free, only to realize that she was desperately thirsty. When she tried to ask for water, all that came from her throat was a feeble squawk.

Once Louisa's bawling woke her up. Nell wanted to ask her what was wrong, but as soon as she started to croak her question, Louisa just cried harder. Nell didn't always remember where she was. One time she thought she saw the northern lights again, only at eye level this time, the shimmering colors close to her face. Then she saw that they were simply icicles with the firelight through them. Another time, when Louisa's sobs penetrated the baffle of sleep, Nell was sure she could hear the sea. Thinking she must be on the island, Nell fumbled with what she thought was a homespun coverlet. But she dropped into sleep again before she could reach Louisa. When she next awoke, she was clutching hemlock needles. She inhaled the woodland scent with surprise and bafflement.

One day she opened her eyes and knew she was watching Louisa and Peter at the fireplace. Joe, striding up to them, kicked snow out of the way.

Summoning all her strength, Nell announced, "I'm back." At least that was what she meant to say.

Louisa gave her a cup of real tea sweetened with molasses. But she was still forced to drink the other kind of tea that was bitter and made her cough. Afterward, though, it was easier to breathe.

The following day Louisa brought warm water for washing and helped Nell dress in clean clothes. But instead of a skirt, Louisa provided trousers made of muskrat skin and a jacket with an attached hood. At first Nell recoiled from the animal smell. But Louisa was insistent. There was a special beaver edge to go next to Nell's face. Joe had gone a very long way in very bad weather to get these skins for her.

Thinking it must have taken a long time, Nell asked Louisa how many days she had been sick.

"Oh, Nell, days and days and days. First Joe was going to take you to a doctor. Only the snow got so bad, we couldn't go. We had to dig a grave here before the ground got all hard. We covered it with branches to keep the snow out."

"You were going to bury me here?"

Louisa nodded. "With stones on top to keep the animals off. Joe made the warm things big in case you died, so they'd fit me."

"You don't have fur clothes like these?"

Louisa shook her head. "Not yet. He's making some now. Rabbit skin. It's hard to hunt in so much snow. We had to eat the last two chickens. Did you like the broth? I made it."

Nell nodded, although she had no recollection of it. It struck her that Louisa didn't sound the same. There was an air of authority in the way she spoke, even in the way she moved. Catching the moose, Louisa jerked his head down to remove the halter. Rubbing it with bear fat, she explained to Nell that everything had to be greased. That was part of getting ready to move on. "The moose is especially bad," Louisa pointed out, "because he keeps digging through the snow with his nose. Then the rawhide gets wet and stiff and rubs him sore." She slapped the moose away from the shelter's spruce boughs and enticed him to the grave to browse on what remained of its covering.

Peter, greasing Seesur's harness, said, "Watch out he doesn't fall in."

Louisa pulled branches out from under the snow so the moose and horse would see the hole. Nell saw it, too—her grave. She wanted to do something useful, to confirm being alive, but the slightest effort started her coughing and prompted Peter to snap at her to sit still.

That night Joe carried her to the loaded sleigh and covered her with the bearskin. Later Peter left the fire to make sure she wasn't cold. But only her nose felt the sting of the bitter air. Lingering, Peter suddenly blurted, "When you almost died, I thought you were the last friend I'd ever have."

"You still had Joe. And Louisa."

He looked at her through the spokes of one of the wheels that had been lashed to the sides of the sleigh. "That's different. You were like my friends in the asylum. *My* friends." He dug his fingers into the dense black fur. "Everything's gone wrong."

Nell said, "We shouldn't be here like this. We should have written Mrs. Fowler. We could have gone on the train. It's been wrong from the start."

"Grandfather had to. He was running away."

"I know."

"Running away from the police, too. He killed that man."

In spite of being warm, Nell shivered. "I know. It's such an awful thing. But you should have told me before. Why didn't you?"

"I was afraid."

"Of your grandfather?"

Peter shook his head. "I was afraid he'd get caught. That's why we had to cross the border so quick. The Canadian police wouldn't follow him."

"Then after that, why didn't he stay on the road?"

"Because the other two robbers might have been looking for

him. Grandfather thought he'd be safer. He knows the woods." Peter faltered.

"Still, here we are, in the woods. All this time." Nell's voice dropped. "I've wondered whether he ever really means for us to get to Pawnook."

"Of course he does," Peter declared hotly. "It's almost all he thinks of, showing Jessie Fowler she was wrong about him, bringing her the cradle. If we hadn't had all this early bad snow, we'd have been in Pawnook long before now. We all want to get there. Jessie can help Grandfather. She'll want to when she learns that he was trying to find you when he killed that man."

Nell stiffened. "He didn't have to kill him, though. He had all the guns. The man was asleep."

Peter let out a long sigh. "You talk like Grandfather. He says no one can help him, not even Jessie, because it will come down to an Indian's word against the white men's."

Nell fell silent then, pondering the tangle of rights and wrongs that bound them all together. It was worse than being shipwrecked and adrift in the fog. You didn't know who you should hold on to, who you could count on.

Peter went on. "I asked Grandfather about what Cookee and Boss mentioned. I asked him what happened on the river. He wouldn't talk about it."

"You think it has to do with the man he killed?"

Peter nodded. "There was already bad feeling between them. I wish he'd tell me."

Nell agreed. "I don't like secrets. I don't like keeping things from Louisa, either, but I don't dare tell her about your grandfather."

"She's bound to find out," Peter commented.

"I know. Only not yet. She's not ready." But as soon as she had spoken, Nell saw that it might not be Louisa who wasn't ready. She snuggled down under the bearskin. If only she could fall asleep and not wake up until this journey was over.

When the moon rose, they were on their way. At first the bobsleigh tipped so wildly, Nell was jounced awake. Only the wheels raised up on either side kept her from being bumped off. Then the sleigh gained the snow-covered ice and all was smooth and quiet.

Even under the night sky, and in spite of being caged between the wheel sides, she could see the world opening out around her. Louisa was allowed to ride on the sleigh for now, but in the morning she had to follow along behind, floundering to keep up.

Joe led the way; the moose brought up the rear. Sometimes he stopped or wandered in another direction. But he always galloped back, looking for all the world like an exaggerated Louisa, loose-jointed, splayed.

Crossing the pond, they came to another like it, and then one the size of a huge lake. The bobs slid easily, whisking the sled so fast that Louisa fell behind. Nell had to call ahead to Joe, who took pity on Louisa and let her ride again.

"It's not fair," she complained. "Joe and Peter have snowshoes."

"Look at the mountains," Nell said to distract her. She pointed beyond the shoreline, above the green-and-black trees and the reddish-tinged branches that brushed the sky with softer tones. On the horizon, stark and cold, a range of mountains seemed to tip the world toward them. "Look," Nell repeated, herself enthralled.

But as soon as they reached the shore, Joe insisted that Louisa get down and walk. The going would be hard enough through these woods.

After the spaciousness and light, the darkness of the trees was almost unbearable. Giant pines towered over the spruce and birch and blocked most of the sky. It was stop and start for Seesur, the snow concealing blow-downs and boulders in his path. But Louisa could almost keep up with him.

When they stopped finally, Joe left Nell on the sleigh until the fire was going and supper started. Louisa helped Nell with her clothes and even supported her a little way off for privacy. It almost seemed to Nell as though she and Louisa had changed places. Louisa was strong, glowing with high spirits and windburn, while Nell could barely totter a few steps on her own.

That night Peter and Joe slept beneath the sleigh, Louisa and Nell snug under the bearskin on top of the load. Louisa groaned with exhaustion and fell sound asleep at once. Nell lay warm enough but wide awake, listening to the wind howling in the treetops.

The next day was slow going. When they stopped to rest, Louisa's cheeks were bright red, her lips cracked, her eyes weepy, but she didn't complain, didn't even seem to notice. By nightfall she had eaten all the mush and meat Joe gave her, gnawing the gristle with relish and licking every speck of fat from her fingers. Nell couldn't swallow the greasy bear meat. She ate a little of the cornmeal mush until it grew cold and stuck in her throat.

"See that?" Louisa said to Nell, pointing to a tree trunk with a figure carved on it.

Nell looked at the picture cut in the bark.

"It's a hunting sign from a long time ago. The People of the Black Cat used to hunt here. Joe told me that."

"It might be one of his stories."

Louisa shook her head. "Before this there were turtle signs. We're in new country now."

Later Nell had a chance to ask Peter about it. "Are we lost?"

"Not at all. Grandfather says we'll be on the river in a day or so."

"He told Louisa we're in another country," Nell countered.

"She doesn't always understand what he's saying," Peter reminded Nell.

On they went, fighting the cold wind and the drifting snow, until they reached the river and were faced with a new problem. The wind swept over the ice with such force, it blew the snow cover away to the banks. Even with the caulks on his shoes, Seesur slipped and stumbled and made little headway downriver. Joe went on ahead to test the footing. When he returned, his face was set in discouragement. It was snowing again, which might eventually improve the surface, but he couldn't risk getting them trapped on the ice without shelter.

He took them to a riverboat he had seen farther along. It was already tipped on its side and lashed between trees on the bank, which meant someone before them had used it as a shelter. The horse and moose were each given a generous feed of oats and then set loose.

Nell worried that they would stray too far. Why not feed them hay so they would stay near? Peter told her the hay would only be blown away; they'd get hardly any.

"This terrible wind," Nell said. "I hate it."

"Wind," Joe informed her, "is First Voice. Voice of Wind-Blower sitting on rock at end of sky in far north."

"Tell," Louisa begged, squatting beside him.

"Told once already," Joe said. "Sit against boat here."

They sat in a row with the boat at their backs.

"Nell doesn't know, though," Louisa pressed. "That's why she minds. Tell her."

Joe portioned out frozen meat. He didn't dare open the cornmeal. A fire was out of the question.

"*N'karnayoo*," he intoned.

"That means 'Of Old Time,'" Louisa translated for Nell.

"*N'karnayoo*," Joe repeated, adding, "*Wood-enit-atokhagen*."

"A story of Glooskeb," Peter put in.

"Finally," Joe commented, "you remember."

"Remembering isn't believing," Peter retorted.

Joe said nothing to this. Turning, Nell looked into his face. His eyes were shut against the blizzard. There was a stillness about him that reminded her of the night of the northern lights.

Finally he began to speak. "When Glooskeb still with People, he went hunting water fowl, got caught in storm. Killed no birds that day. So he went to Wind-Blower, tells him to be easy with his wings for the sake of his grandchildren, the People. But Wind-Blower say, 'I am here since oldest time. I move my wings. Mine is First Voice. I will not stop.' Then Glooskeb take Wind-Blower like duck, tie his wings, throw him in rocky gorge. So there is no wind at all. People can go out in canoes every day. Only water dead, stinking, soon so thick, not even Glooskeb can paddle on it. So back to Wind-Blower, pick him up, untie one wing, and put him back on rock. Since then winds never so terrible. This is end of story."

Nell said, "Wind-Blower must have got the other wing free to make this wind."

Joe shook his head. "Seen worse."

"Anyway," Peter declared, "there's nothing you can do about it except wait it out."

"You can pray," Louisa reminded him.

Peter laughed. "To Wind-Blower?"

Nell spoke up then. "Of course not. To God, that's who."

"Don't you know we're in a God-forsaken land?" He shrugged himself down under the buffalo robe. "How far do you think your prayer will go? The wind catches everything, every word."

Mind-bruised and battered by the shrieking bird of the north, Nell couldn't think of a reply.

But Louisa asserted that God hears your prayer wherever you are. She turned to Nell. "Don't you believe that?"

Nell said she supposed so. To her surprise Joe agreed.

"Many times when I am young I say Our Father. Then I believe He hear. Now I think maybe some stories like ones of Old Time. Jesus walk on water maybe when it frozen or full of logs. Still, I remember story. Important to remember best you can, even without clover."

"Clover?"

"That's the Indian memory," Peter told her. "Every newborn child was supposed to be fed white clover crushed in clear water to give it memory for life. Of course, Grandfather is convinced that no one fed it to me. And since I can't remember when I was newborn, I guess that's proof that I lacked the clover start. It doesn't bother me, but Grandfather minds."

The wind howled and shrieked. Occasional gusts toppled snowdrifts and blew the loose snow right at them. But mostly the boat protected them as they huddled under the buffalo robe and the bearskin.

Joe said, "White clover follows every man's footsteps."

Louisa said, "What if we all pray at the same time? Then maybe God will hear us."

"What will we pray for?" Peter sounded angry. "We have food. We're not lost. Isn't that right, Grandfather?"

Nell could feel Joe turn toward Peter, who was on the far side of Louisa. Joe had to lean across Nell to speak to him. But Nell missed every word. Wind-Blower was on top of Joe's voice the moment he let it go.

19/Calling Moose

For a while the storm's brightness deceived them into believing the worst was over. Here was light; here, somewhere beyond the translucent whirl of snow, the sun. Yet the wind picked up again and flayed them with ice. They didn't try to talk or to move. In time they slept.

When Nell awoke, the storm really was winding down. Snow clung to every root and branch; it lay in rippling windrows across the river ice.

Louisa asked about Seesur and the moose. Joe said they might be stuck awhile before they could work their way back through the drifts. Louisa scowled. They would freeze; they would starve. But Joe assured her that moose wintered in these woods every year. There had been many moose in this country before the sportsmen came. That gave Louisa something else to worry about. Would some hunter shoot their moose? Joe said he doubted it. Most sporters only wanted moose with a full rack of antlers. Joe spread his arms wide to show her what he meant.

"Then it might be an Indian hunter," Louisa insisted.

Joe shrugged, letting her know that was possible. "Anyway," he told her, "we close now, soon there."

It seemed to Nell that he said something like that whenever he wanted to change the subject. "How do you know?" she challenged.

"The river. One time it run north. White man turned it around, dams there and there. Now river runs logs south to mills, to ships."

"You mean, you really have been here before?" To know this warmed Nell much more than the feeble flame Joe nursed along.

Joe nodded. "Big changes. That way slate and iron." He nodded downriver and across. "All very tall trees most gone. Caribou gone, too, with trees."

They spent the day digging out firewood. Nell tried to pick up sticks from a drop point and carry them the last stretch of well-packed snow to the boat shelter, but her legs kept caving in.

"You'll get sick again," Louisa told her. "Stay by the fire." Joe had bound a basket to her back with a strap around her forehead and waist, and she trudged back and forth, Indian fashion, leaning into the weight.

Secretly Nell was glad that Seesur and the moose took their time returning. Eager as she was to reach Pawnook, she was exhausted and chilled and grateful for the fire and the bearskin. For the first time since her illness, the cornmeal mush and meat tasted good. That evening she fell asleep before dark, feeling better, feeling hopeful.

She woke to Louisa's loud protest. "I didn't think you'd mind."

"You took my snowshoes," Peter railed. "That's the dumbest thing anyone could do, except that time Nell went into the snow."

"Louisa took your snowshoes?" Nell sat up. "She wouldn't steal."

"I borrowed them," Louisa yelled. "I was looking for Seesur and the moose. I just went to find them."

"At least," said Peter, "it was easy to track her down." He turned on Louisa again. "Did you ever think there might've been another moose or bear? What about hungry wolves?"

Louisa ran to meet Joe, who had stopped at the sleigh to bring cornmeal for their breakfast. "Do wolves eat moose?"

"Sometimes. Sometimes in deep snow."

Louisa's face screwed up. She began to cry.

"Oh, be quiet," Peter ordered. "Wolves would eat you first. You make so much noise, they'd have an easy time finding you."

"Won't get moose like that," Joe told her.

To Nell's amazement, Louisa gulped back her sobs.

Joe nodded. "Better. Show you now how to call moose. You see." He strode off toward a grove of yellow birch.

Louisa tumbled down in the shelter beside Nell.

"How far did you get?" Nell asked her.

"Pretty far. It's easier with snowshoes."

"All alone! Were you afraid?"

"Not alone," Louisa responded. "God was with me. He showed me a palace."

"Louisa, there aren't any palaces in the woods."

Louisa blew on her hands. "Well, it didn't have tall things or lots of rooms, but it was a palace, anyway. It had curtains and pictures on the ceiling and lamps with dangly things and glass and gold and big mirrors."

"You know what that sounds like?" Nell said gently. "It sounds like a dream. Anyway," she added, "I'm glad you're brave, and I'm glad you're back and safe."

Louisa sighed. "I used to be afraid of the trees. I thought they were giants. I thought they walked at me. Now I know they're just trees with different names. Every part of them has something you can use, like bark for medicine tea and roots for thread. But Joe says in the Old Time they really were giants, so I wasn't wrong before, either." She paused. "And I'm not wrong about the palace."

Nell gave in then. Louisa was on the verge of sleep. Nell pulled the bearskin over her head and waited for the warmth to come.

It was a waiting day. Louisa slept most of the morning. Joe stitched birch bark into a cone shape. He plied together root fibers from his bag to make a thread. In the evening he showed Louisa the moose horn he had made, but when she raised the small end to her mouth, he whipped it out of her hands. Stung, she blinked at him. He told her it was not for play.

Peter asked if it wasn't too late in the season for calling moose. Joe said he might still fool a young moose, although an older one would be unlikely to respond to a call past rutting time. He launched into another Glooskeb story.

Louisa prodded Nell. "Glooskeb could call any animal anytime." But Nell was sleepy. For the first time since her illness she had cooked for them, a stew with bear meat and frozen potatoes that turned mushy in the pot. It didn't take much to drain her, and Joe's story came to her only as a lulling cadence.

For an instant she held intact a thought about Glooskeb casting off all the creatures and how they had lost their song then, their memory. A line from a hymn floated up from the past: "God is my strong salvation; what foe have I to fear? . . ." She thought she saw Joe walking away, Louisa in a trance following him. "No, no," she cried, shaken awake. Dazed, she sought light. But it was still dark. Joe's whisper came to her: "Keep still now. I call moose."

"I was dreaming," she murmured. "I was afraid."

"Stay." He pressed her down under the stiff bearskin. "Stay warm."

She heard his soft footsteps scuffing through the snow, then listened to the intense silence of the frozen woods. The first call from downriver was so unearthly, it sent shivers all through her. It sounded like the bray of a wounded animal. When it began again, she heard the shape of it, long, rasping notes followed by short, descending grunts. Then silence, until the cry erupted all over again.

Peter sat up. Louisa, on her elbow, tried to keep covered. Finally, from far off, they heard a kind of echo, a muted honking that fell away in muffled groans.

When Joe reappeared, Nell saw him at first as an indistinct figure, a dark shape moving over the snow-covered ice. He might have been Glooskeb himself calling the first creatures into the world.

Joe shredded the moose call to start their fire. "Smoke help moose find way. Horse, too," he said. He threw snow in the kettle, and when it melted, he added more. They had hot tea with molasses before sunup. They huddled under the bearskin and the buffalo robe, but the cold came up from beneath them, right through the spruce branches. Nell was dozing when Joe suddenly, quietly spoke. "There!"

The moose and Seesur, breaking through the snow crust, scrambled up the riverbank, stopped at the sleigh, and nudged the rubber blanket.

Louisa threw aside the bearskin and dashed out to them. Nell rolled into the warm spot she left. A little later Louisa returned, flinging herself down beside Nell again and babbling with relief. She hugged Nell, who shuddered in her icy embrace. Nell was only released after she agreed with Louisa that they were the luckiest girls in the world because they had Joe, who could call animals from the wild darkness.

20/Louisa's Palace

A t midday the sun reappeared for a while, bringing the comfort of its beauty but not much warmth. The moose and the horse stood out on the river to get the full benefit of its rays until the wind drove them back to the trees. To keep them close, Joe fed them precious cornmeal. Tonight, he said, would be the coldest time of all. He pointed to white spots on Peter's cheeks and made him stay by the fire. Then Joe went searching for hickory wood because it burned more slowly than any other. When he came back without any, he tethered Seesur and the moose behind the tilted boat.

Everyone huddled together the way they had at the storm's full fury. This time, though, the bitter air was still. They needed only to whisper for their voices to carry. Nell wondered where the birds had gone. Where were the squirrels and rabbits? The moon slid over the white crust, lighting every twig, every frozen lump and ripple. Nothing moved upon that barren surface.

In the morning Joe broiled bear steak and insisted that everyone eat as much as possible. Nell gave Seesur a feed of cornmeal in his nose bag. Louisa did the same for the moose. Then it was time to hitch up. Joe let the girls ride on the bobsleigh while he and Peter led the way downriver.

The moose came weaving in and out of the trees, never losing sight of Seesur but stopping to hunt for dead weeds at the edge of the river. Sometimes he stretched his short neck and searched out a shred of bark with his loose, overhanging lip.

Nell couldn't help commenting on him. "There couldn't be a stranger-looking animal. Or clumsier," she added as he slithered and plunged through a drift to catch up with them.

"God doesn't think he's ugly," Louisa countered.

"I didn't say he was. Only . . . only Seesur has such kind eyes and a noble head and a beautiful thick mane."

"The moose has a mane on top and another underneath. Anyway," Louisa declared, looking down at her lap, "God loves all the creatures, even if they're not clever or pretty."

"You're right," Nell quickly assured her.

Louisa raised her eyes then. Looking all around, she tried to stand up and shout ahead to Joe. "Stop! My palace! It's that way, on the other side of the river. Stop, we're passing it!"

"Passing what?" Peter called back.

Nell said, "Louisa thought she saw a . . . palace in the woods."

"I did, I did," Louisa insisted. She scrambled off the sleigh.

"It's nothing," Peter shouted to his grandfather. "Just Louisa being silly."

But Joe returned to them. He listened first to Louisa, next to Peter and Nell, who knew better than to believe such nonsense.

"Better go look," Joe decided.

"Another delay?" Peter protested.

The moose surged past them and took off across the river. "That way, yes," Louisa argued.

Joe sent Peter after the moose. He made Louisa get back on the sleigh. Then he set out in Peter's tracks. Seesur seemed to want to go, too. He took one step, then a few more, pawing the snowy ice.

Joe had just reached the far riverbank when Peter's shout stopped him. Seesur stole a few more steps; he started to neigh. Nell couldn't hear what Peter was telling Joe, but she could see that they were excited.

Cupping her hands to her mouth, she called across the ice. "What is it?"

Peter, returning now beside his grandfather, pointed back into the trees. "A wreck. A train." When he came closer, he added, "Louisa was right."

"You saw my palace?"

"There's an engine down the gully, the tender with it, and two boxcars, one up but tilted, one down. There's another car standing. It's . . . it's what Louisa said. Only," he finished, turning to her, "you didn't mention it was a railroad car."

Louisa, looking embarrassed, said, "I didn't see any engine. I was only there a moment. I looked in through the window on the door. Then I heard you coming for me, and you sounded mad, so I went to meet you."

"You should have told me."

"I tried to. You wouldn't listen. Then, when you yelled at me for stealing your snowshoes that I'd just borrowed, I didn't feel like telling you anything."

"We go," Joe announced.

"Can't we wait for the moose?" Louisa pleaded.

"Moose maybe there already. You see."

Joe was right. The moose had broken a path through the deep snow. But it was a struggle for Seesur to haul the sleigh over the uneven drifts. The girls plunged and wallowed behind.

They came upon the standing car so suddenly that Nell, her head down, her arms spread for balance, almost walked into the back of the sleigh. Louisa was already scrambling ahead and mounting the platform to peer inside.

Joe made them wait while he looked and touched and then finally raised the lever to wrench the door open. Then he waved them in. By the time Nell struggled up the snowy steps, Peter and Louisa were ranging all over, stroking the green velvet curtains, testing the plush seats, and fingering the polished wood.

"A washroom," Peter reported from the far end. "I've never seen a railroad car like this before."

"You never saw a palace, either," Louisa responded.

Nell found her voice. "Don't touch anything. It's not ours. It might break."

Peter burst out laughing. "Break? It's been in a wreck!" He

walked toward her, flourishing a glass goblet. Then he took aim at his own reflection in a mirrored partition.

"Put it down," Joe commanded. "You break, you pay. Anything."

Sullenly Peter set the goblet on a table. "I was only joking," he muttered. But Nell thought he would have smashed it and the mirror just to prove that he wasn't intimidated by all this elegance.

After Joe examined the stove he sent everyone out for wood. Thick, gray flakes wafted out of the dull sky. The sun had faded to a dingy yellow stain.

Nell kept expecting the railroad car to vanish like the sun, like a dream at daybreak. She could understand how it had looked to Louisa like a palace. The snow-peaked roof overlying the mustard-yellow sides gave it a kind of splendor that could dazzle anyone accustomed to the woods for weeks and weeks. The color was almost violent, the red-and-black decorations seen through snow too bold and brilliant to be real.

Peter returned from unhitching Seesur to report that the boxcar lying on its side contained hay. "And you should see the engine!" he told Nell. "Well, most of it's covered with snow, but you can see one red wheel. Bright red!"

The wind picked up, dashing flakes against the car, against Nell's face. The snow turned to beads of stinging ice. It was hard to find wood, and harder still to move it. Joe set Nell to work on the bobsleigh collecting bear meat, two whole rabbits, cornmeal, and potatoes. Everything was frozen hard. Clutching them felt like hugging cakes of ice.

The wind blew gobs of overhanging snow from the roof of the train. Turning from the sleigh, Nell read the bold letters that ran the length of the car: NORTHERN LIGHTS. It was just a name emblazoned on the lurid paint. It had nothing to do with the pulsing blues and greens that had shivered the night sky and set the pond ablaze.

Later, in the vestibule, where everyone shed their soaked outerwear, the animal odor from all the wet skins was nearly over-powering. Peter and Louisa led the way through the car. They passed a desk and chairs, sleeping partitions, a walled-off kitchen compartment, and arrived in the dining area where the stove was. Nell, behind them, kept her arms tight against her sides, but Peter reached up as he went along to drag down blankets from an open upper berth. The windows at the dining-parlor end were already steamed up.

Nell walked into the washroom and closed the door. The lavish indoor warmth had not yet penetrated this small compartment; snow-light entered through the one high-up window. She started to leave, but Joe met her in the doorway with a pail of warm water. She saw another pail beside the stove with long icicles sticking out of it.

Back in the washroom, Nell pulled off her blouse and stepped out of the rest of her sodden things. Pouring warm water into the basin, she bathed herself from head to toe. Before she was finished, Louisa joined her, squealing with delight when her turn came. Now even their window filmed over. Nell eyed the lamp beside the mirror. There was kerosene, a wick, and matches in a glass jar. Did she dare to use up fuel belonging to some important railway company?

"But it's an answer to a prayer," she murmured, reaching toward the matches, then checking herself.

"It is," Louisa agreed. "It's exactly what I prayed for in the storm. We can live happily ever after now."

"Oh, no, Louisa," Nell exclaimed with a laugh, "not here. Not in a train."

"Why not?" Louisa demanded, and then gave way to laughter, too, because it was, after all, a joke. No one lived in a train in the middle of the woods. Even Louisa, scrubbed and warm and wrapping herself in the clean blanket, didn't have to be told what nonsense that was.

21/A Mountain Named Joe?

That night Nell and Louisa shared an upper berth. They slept between sheets under soft, sweet-smelling wool blankets. Outside the palace car, the wind shrieked. Nell thought of Wind-Blower beating his unbound wing. She could see Joe stretched out on the sofa, a flicker of light from the stove revealing his hat on his chest. She tugged aside the washed clothes that hung in front of the berth. Since they felt dry, she pulled them free and let them drop with a muted thud to the carpet. Then, very quietly, she pulled the bed curtains closed. The berth became a tiny room of their own.

Overnight their lives had been transformed. Except for going out to squat in the lee of the train, because Joe would not let them use the closeted toilet, the girls remained inside. They were dry. They weren't cold. It was wonderful.

Joe and Peter checked on the animals and decided to try to board up the boxcar to keep the horse and moose out of it. An uncovered boxcar tipped on its side full of hay was too inviting. Joe was afraid they would spoil and waste the precious hay. But he had to give up while the storm raged. The wind blew too hard to hold anything in place, and the animals were right on top of them.

Joe and Peter dragged more wood to the palace car and brought some in to dry.

"Look at the carpet!" Nell cried in dismay, the hairbrush in her hand.

"Look at Louisa," Peter retorted.

Turning, Nell saw Louisa, who had just squirmed out of reach of the brush with a ruffled lamp shade perched on her head.

"Louisa, put that back," Nell snapped. "This is a special car. We have to set everything to rights here before we leave. Let me finish getting the snarls out of your hair."

"In the kitchen," Louisa wheedled. "Then I can look at things while you're hurting me."

There was hardly room enough for both of them there. Only half the width of the car, the kitchen was full of gadgets like tip bins, trays, and drawers containing utensils. While Nell brushed the tangled curls, Louisa rummaged in every nook and cranny and came upon a small packet of white sugar and a sack of rice. Nell set them over the drain in the tiny sink. Digging deep in the pan closet, Louisa cried out in triumph.

"What are they?" she asked, holding up three glass jars.

Nell was excited, too. "Raisins and almonds," she said, recalling the Satterlee pantry. "And I think that one has barley in it. No, tapioca. It's for puddings."

"Puddings!" crowed Louisa.

Later they had tea in china cups while Joe and Peter discussed what railway this might be and where the train had been heading. Joe was puzzled. If this was a new branch line, it bore no resemblance to the kind of train used for carrying slate from a quarry or iron from a forge.

"If only we could see the tracks," Peter said.

"You can guess where they go from the way the woods are cut for them."

Nell, stirring the tapioca pudding and dropping thawed raisins into it, recalled the night she had waited in the woods all alone. It had comforted her to think that she might follow the tracks back to Woodville. At this moment she didn't really care where these tracks came from or led to. All that mattered was that they represented civilization. As soon as the storm let up, they could follow the tracks to the nearest town or road and ask the way to Paw-nook.

The storm lasted three days. Midway, there was a lull, but the wind was only gathering force from the east. It slammed into the car and piled up drifts that made going outside almost impossible.

Louisa fussed because they couldn't see the horse and the moose. They might be frozen by now.

"You know how long their hair is," Nell said to her. "They're wearing their winter coats."

"We could put blankets on them, too," Louisa pressed.

"You're bothering Joe," Peter said to hush her.

Joe sat on the carpet, his back against the sofa, his knees drawn up.

Louisa's voice dropped. "He's thinking a story."

"He doesn't like being cooped up like this," Peter remarked, keeping his voice very low. He went on whittling in silence, and then added, "He might be worrying about food. Of course, we still have the moose to eat."

"No," Louisa wailed.

"You didn't have to do that," Nell whispered to Peter.

Louisa dashed to Joe and kneeled in front of him. "You won't kill him. He's my friend."

Joe, sounding distant, told her they still had some bear meat.

"And you can hunt if you need to," she prompted.

"Bad hunting now. You see."

"If we're almost there," Louisa insisted, "we won't need much more."

"Maybe," Joe answered.

Nell wondered whether he meant maybe they were almost home or maybe they wouldn't need much more meat. Still cross with Peter for taunting Louisa, Nell snapped at him about getting shavings all over the carpet.

"There'll be more mess than this to clean up before we're out of here," he returned evenly.

"What do you mean? We're not stopping here any longer than we have to."

He rubbed the stick he was whittling. "You think we're going anywhere in this weather?"

"The storm will end. It can't last much longer." Why didn't he answer? Why couldn't he just agree with her?

Louisa said, "I like it here. I don't mind staying." Getting up, she set the table with porcelain and glass and silver. Then she rearranged the cutlery. Presenting and removing soup bowls, she muttered an occasional word, a scrap of conversation with invisible diners. Suddenly she swept her arm in a grand gesture that knocked a goblet to the carpet.

Nell lunged for it and warned Louisa that if it broke, she would have to pay for it.

Arrested, Louisa frowned. "How? Pay who?"

"Oh, I don't know, you just would." Stalking to the other end of the car, Nell dropped into the desk chair with her back to all of them.

She stared at the blotting paper on the desk, at the empty grooves for pens. Toying with the inkwell, she found the ink frozen. The heat from the stove didn't reach far enough to melt it. Idly she pulled open the top drawer. There was real paper and a cigar box full of pens. The next drawer contained a ledger and, underneath it, two books. "Oh!" she exclaimed with joy. Behind them she found a kind of newspaper.

Peter and Louisa came quickly. Peter picked up the newspaper, then dropped it with disgust. "It's not even this year," he said. Glancing at the masthead, Nell read: *The Transcontinental.* It was dated May 24, 1870. She read far enough to see that it was published by an excursion sponsored by the Boston Board of Trade. This issue was printed in Niagara Falls on a train that would go all the way across the country to San Francisco. Slipping it back into the drawer, she turned to the books.

With a thrill of excitement she opened *David Copperfield* to the first page and read aloud. "'Whether I shall turn out to be the hero of my own life, or whether that station will be held by anybody else, these pages must show. . . .'"

"Go on," Louisa prompted.

"'To begin my life with the beginning of my life, I record that I was born (as I have been informed and believe) on a Friday at twelve o'clock at night. . . .'"

"Think of knowing that much about yourself," Louisa remarked.

Peter picked up the other book and stared at the cover. "Henry," he read, then "David." He showed it to Nell, who said, "That's the author, Henry David Thoreau. It's called *The Allegash and East Branch*."

"What's it about?"

Nell couldn't tell from just a quick glance through the pages. She read aloud, "'From this dead water the outlines around the mountains of Ktaadn were visible. The top of Ktaadn was concealed by a cloud, but . . .'" Stumbling over a word she couldn't pronounce, she skipped to "'We steered across the northwest end of the lake, from which we looked down south-southeast, the whole length to Joe Merry Mountain, seen over its extremity.'"

"A mountain named Joe?" Louisa exclaimed.

"I suppose so." Nell read some more. "'It is one of the surprises which nature has in store for the traveler in the forest. To look down, in this case, over eighteen miles of water, was liberating and civilizing even. No doubt, the short distance to which you can see in the woods, and the general twilight, would at length react on the inhabitants, and make them salvages.'" She handed the book to Peter. "Savages," she repeated. "That's us, at least until we came here."

Peter laughed. "Savages, yes. That's us. Indians."

Nell took *David Copperfield* back to read beside the stove. Peter brought the Allegash book along with him, leafing through it as he listened to Nell.

Joe sat through the reading aloof, unmoving. From time to time Nell glanced his way to make sure she wasn't disturbing him. Even though he didn't seem to be listening to her, she couldn't rid herself of his brooding presence.

When she paused to give her voice a rest, Louisa and Peter stretched out their feet to the stove and waited quietly for her to go on. Instead of sharing their peace and pleasure, it was Joe's somber mood she felt, his stillness like ice over thunderous rapids. To keep her grip on the smooth surface of the moment she pushed on, her voice going hoarse. "'I am glad to recollect that when the carrier began to move, my mother ran out at the gate, and called to him to stop, that she might kiss me once more.'"

Nell heard Louisa sniffling. Without knowing anything of life with parents, the image of David Copperfield leaving home for the first time had made her cry. Nell's eyes prickled, too. Even Peter had to clear his throat. No one was left untouched by the sadness of this separation. Except Joe, of course.

Nell stole another look at him. All of a sudden it came to her that he had lost a son on the river. Shivering, she faltered.

"Go on," Louisa commanded.

"Later," Nell told her. "This is enough for now." She wished Peter could find the courage to ask Joe what had happened on the river.

Louisa went into the kitchen. Nell heard her rattling pans and clicking spoons. Peter, the other book in hand, withdrew to his berth.

Nell waited a moment. It was she who needed to gather her courage, to ask what Peter was unable to speak to his grandfather about. Nell swiveled around, drawing closer to Joe. She drew a breath.

"The lumber-camp boss said things about you. About the river." Joe stirred. His eyes met hers. She was afraid to mention his son before he did. "Won't you say what happened? Shouldn't

Peter know?" She guessed that Peter was still staring at the book in his hands; she knew he must be listening.

"Maybe. Maybe so." Joe spoke haltingly. "That time gone."

How could it ever be gone for Joe? "Was it Peter's uncle?" she asked. "His mother's brother?"

Joe nodded. Peter, the book still in hand, slid off the berth.

"An accident?" Nell prompted softly.

"On river." Joe stared at his feet. "Long time ago."

Louisa called from the kitchen, "Is this a story of the Old Time?"

Peter whipped around. "No. Be quiet."

Joe picked at a thread from his sleeve and rolled it on his knee the way he plied root threads to make them strong.

"A long time ago on the river," Nell reminded him.

He nodded once more. "Dead Man's Pitch bad, bad water. Kill many men, that place. This man, he say to Tomah, to my son, he say only white men in boat. Why no Indian dare go with them, take boat down rapids? So Tomah, he get in boat with them white men."

"Why didn't you stop him?" Peter demanded.

Joe shook his head. "I'm downriver. Logs jammed at first pitch. Working there. Someone say, 'Better get them logs free. Boat's coming.'"

Peter said, "So you didn't know he was in the boat?"

"That right. Saw boat coming. Logs go sudden, like dam open. That boat . . ." Leaning forward, Joe picked up a sliver of wood from Peter's whittling and flicked it into the air. "Like that. River toss him boat right over. All loose logs coming, too."

"What about you?" Nell asked. "Where were you?"

"Running logs. On way to shore, nearly there."

"So you turned back," Peter put in, "because your son Tomah was there in the boat."

"Didn't see Tomah. Only see fools flapping in water. One there, logs roll right over, him gone under. Another grab log shooting downriver. Found him later, miles on."

"What about Tomah?"

"I run fast across logs to upside-down boat. Turn boat over, find Tomah underneath. Drag him and one other into boat, both dead. Still one more in water, yelling for me to catch him. I try to hold boat, grab tree roots, hold tight, and reach for man in river. Now men coming with ropes and poles. Hold on, hold on. River coming, logs coming, men with ropes coming. Have this man like drowning dog." Joe showed them with his good hand, as if pulling a dog by the scruff of its neck. "This is man who dared Tomah into boat, but I don't know this then. Hold him man. Logs come first, push boat, slam together fingers around root. Still hold him. Then men with ropes haul us out of way of logs, me, Joe Pennowit, and this man who make the trouble. No one want him after that. No one give him work." Joe rubbed his mutilated hand. "No work on river anymore for Joe, either."

"Was he the man who came with the others to Gabe Fowler?"

Joe nodded. "Plenty surprised when I show up."

Peter set his book aside. "Considering what he did, I don't see how he could blame you for telling Gabe to send him away."

Stretching, Joe stood up. "Maybe blame me because I save him life."

Peter scowled. "That doesn't make sense."

Joe walked to the end of the car before he turned to answer. "What make sense," he declared, pulling his knife from its sheath and holding it high, "is this." His hand started to descend. Then abruptly he returned the knife to the sheath.

Only Nell recoiled. Only Nell could see those three men asleep on the ground, see Joe describing in one swift, downward thrust what he had done.

Bracing against the wind as he backed out, Joe held the stump against his chest. For one instant it looked to Nell as though the mutilated hand was not fingerless, only clenched in a hard, angry fist.

22/Mighty One

After the storm Joe boarded up the boxcar to keep the horse and moose from devouring the hay all at once. Then he went off to hunt by himself. When he returned without game, he didn't speak of it. He just set his rifle down and went to the stove to warm his hands.

Nell, who was reading aloud, fell silent. Louisa darted an anxious glance at Joe, then at Nell, then at Joe again. She went to peer out the window in the direction of the boxcar. Nell could see that she was frightened for the moose.

"Listen, Louisa." Nell spoke more sharply than she intended. "We're beginning a new chapter. 'I know enough of the world now,'" Nell read, "'to have almost lost the capacity of being much surprised by anything; but it is a matter of some surprise to me, even now, that I can have been so easily thrown away at such an age.'"

"Thrown away," Peter mused. "At least he could do what he chose."

"He was only ten," Nell reminded Peter.

"You were on your own at ten. You were in service."

"Yes, but with the Satterlees, who cared for us."

Peter snorted. "Cared like those Warburton people?"

"No, different."

"We're all thrown away," Peter declared. "My new mother threw me away into that asylum for Indian orphans."

Louisa turned back from the window. "Your own mother did that?"

"Not my real mother."

Nell lay the book facedown on her lap. "I thought you liked the asylum. They were going to teach you railroad work."

"That's true. But being put there was like being thrown away. You, too, in the workhouse."

Nell could feel the heat rise into her face. "I wasn't thrown away. My brother left me there because he couldn't keep me. It was just for a while, but then they put me on a ship for America."

Peter laughed. "You don't call that throwing you away?"

"My brother came back for me." Nell couldn't keep her voice down. "They told him I was lost at sea. He would have taken care of me."

"Joe takes care of us," Louisa put in. She looked at Joe for a response.

Nell could hear Joe's stump hand rasping against the wet fabric of his trousers. She knew that the stump was painful when it was warming up. Without a word Joe stood up, hoisted his rifle onto his shoulder, and went out.

"Where's he going?" cried Louisa. She ran to the window again. "What's he going to do?"

"Oh, sit down," Peter told her irritably. "Can't you see you've driven him out again?"

Louisa appealed to Nell. "I didn't mean to. What did I do?"

Nell's heart went out to her. "We all drive him away. I shouldn't have been so noisy myself. Come and listen to the story."

"I don't want to." Louisa stood disconsolately in the middle of the car. "Most of the time I don't know what's happening in that book."

"Why don't you set the table again? Say the Queen is coming."

"Better make it the President," Peter advised.

"Does the President live in a palace, too?" Louisa asked.

Nell assured her that the President was every bit as grand as the Queen.

"Help me," Louisa wheedled. "I don't know what a President does."

Setting *David Copperfield* aside, Nell joined Louisa at the table. "Peter can be the President," she decided, rippling her fingers through the curtain fringe.

Peter grinned up at her from the carpet. "Fine. Wake me up when breakfast is ready."

She plumped a green cushion with a scene stitched on it and tossed it down to him. "What will you have for breakfast, sir?" she asked him.

"No corn bread," he said. "Ham."

"Pancakes?" Louisa suggested.

Peter raised himself on his elbow. "Yes, and sausages and eggs. And coffee with milk. I mean, cream. And cider."

They dressed the table with all the finery the car could produce. They pretended to bake and fry and set out a breakfast so grand, they needed to invite guests.

"Mrs. Fowler," Nell suggested.

"With the President of the United States?" Peter laughed. "You have to have important people. Kings and company directors. Educated people like that doctor you worked for." He plucked a cushion from the most elegant chair, the one they called the throne. "This here is Mr. Pullman, who makes fancy train cars like this one. He has factories and offices."

Nell propped one of the picture cushions against the table. "This is Mrs. Pullman."

"Ladies don't have breakfast with the President."

"Why not? What about his wife? What about the Queen? She's come for a visit."

Serving the imaginary guests, Louisa stumbled against the bucket of ice melting beside the stove. That reminded them that the animals needed water. They stopped to carry out the bucket, refill it, and bring in more firewood.

It was good to get out. The air seemed a trace milder. But they

had a terrible time getting out some hay without letting the horse and moose into the boxcar. The moose was especially stubborn, leaning and pressing and stretching his short but powerful neck. Peter had to climb up the slanted board, grab the moose's coarse mane, and haul himself onto his angular back. The moose didn't seem to notice until Peter clambered onto the high shoulders, leaned forward, and grabbed the loose skin dangling below the moose's jaw. The moose coughed, shook his head, and finally backed away from the boxcar.

After that they got the boxcar boarded up again. Then Louisa begged for a turn riding the moose. Peter hoisted her up, kicked some hay out to the moose to keep him happy, and started down to the riverbank to get ice.

Nell went along to help Peter fill the bucket and some empty sacks with chunks of ice.

They worked fast to keep their hands from freezing, and were nearly done when they heard Louisa yell. At first Nell thought she was shouting at the moose. But the tone soon changed from alarm to rage and desperation.

"We're coming," Nell called.

Louisa uttered a piercing scream.

"Hold on," Peter shouted.

"I can't," she screeched. "Help!"

It was impossible to run through the deep snow. When they came puffing to the boxcar, they found only Seesur quietly munching hay.

Looking up the embankment, they saw Louisa, plastered with snow, pounding at the hind end of the moose, which seemed to be lodged partly on the platform at the end of the car with one gangly leg sprawled behind.

"Don't let him in there," Nell shouted.

"I'm not," Louisa wailed. "I couldn't stop him. Peter, grab his tail."

Sputtering and gasping, Peter declared the tail too short to hold. "Anyway, that'll just send him forward."

"It's not funny!" Louisa sobbed. "I think he's stuck."

Peter ran all the way to the other end of the car, where there was another door. They hadn't opened it before, and it took a while for him to wrench up the lever. Nell raced after him and followed him through the car. The moose's head projected inside the vestibule. He had managed to jam one leg partly in, but his high shoulders wedged him just that far. Far enough, Nell saw with horror, to allow him to nibble the green fringe on the nearest curtain.

Flying at his head, Peter whacked the bulging nose. The moose rolled an eye at him and continued, delicately but determinedly, to browse on the curtain fringe. "He thinks he's eating grass," Peter sputtered. The moose made a swipe at the tieback, which snapped from its hook and disappeared inside his enormous mouth. Peter dashed into the kitchen. Returning with an iron frying pan, he slammed it against the moose's muzzle. The jaws opened and dropped a slathery green mess onto the carpet.

"Oh, don't hurt him," Nell cried.

"What's Peter doing to him?" Louisa wailed from the other side.

"Out of the way," Peter shouted to her. "Get back or you'll be trampled."

Louisa, her sobs coming from farther off, begged him not to kill the moose.

"If he dies," Peter retorted, "it'll be from a bellyache." He picked up a bit of smoldering wood with the fire tongs and waved it in front of the moose. Some of the hair on his long face sizzled and gave off a nasty smell. Snorting, he tried to throw his head back, but he had no room. Peter moved closer. The moose grunted, coughed, and pulled back. Peter kept right after him until he was no longer connected to the palace car.

Nell and Peter and Louisa surveyed the damage. A lamp had

fallen, leaking kerosene onto the carpet. The curtain nearest the door was in ruins. They decided that Louisa should help finish getting the ice with Peter. That would give Nell a chance to clean the carpet and get rid of the stuff the moose had slobbered. It occurred to her to add to the list she had begun for Joe. There were two columns on the sheet of paper in the top desk drawer, one the debt to the Fowlers, the other to the railroad. Under raisins, almonds, rice, tapioca, and sugar, she wrote, "window shade," because she wasn't sure how to spell curtain.

Joe returned dragging a caribou that he had found already dead upstream. He had to use the ax to chop off meat for the stew pot; the carcass was much too frozen to skin and cut properly. Tomorrow they would hoist it up on the car roof with a rope.

Nell started the stew water boiling and put away the table settings. Thank goodness the moose had got no farther. Think of all the broken glass and china she would have had to add to the list.

Joe had to wait for the caribou chunk to thaw before he could get the skin off. Nell noticed that there was no fat coating. Joe said the bone marrow would serve as fat.

"Hungry time now," he added. "For all animals. Many people, too."

Louisa turned her rosy face to him. "Not for us. You brought food when we needed it. Like calling the moose. You can get anything."

Joe shook his head. "Not call dead caribou."

"Well, I think you can do everything. Like Glooskeb."

"Even Glooskeb can't do everything."

"I thought if he sang his magic song, all the animals had to obey."

"All but," Joe told her.

"It's a story, isn't it? Tell."

Joe rubbed his forehead and combed the hair out of his eyes. "Another time."

Something in his voice, in his gesture, brought Nell up short.

She heard such extreme weariness in him that it sent a pang through her.

"Now," Louisa pleaded. "While the meat is cooking. There's time."

Nell wanted to tell Louisa to leave him in peace, but she knew that would lead to loud protests. All Nell could do was walk away and try to busy herself in the little kitchen.

Joe sat awhile. When he finally spoke, his words dragged. "Of Old Time. This is story of Glooskeb."

Nell, surrounded by things of new time—a can opener, a spatula, a colander—found herself listening for the next words.

"When Glooskeb conquered all spirits of night, all big things in land and sea and sky, a woman of the People told him there was yet One other, and that One would stay unconquered to end of time."

Louisa sucked in her breath. Nell hoped Peter would give her a warning nudge. If she interrupted now, she might drive Joe outside for the third time that day.

Joe went on. "Woman pointed to baby sitting on ground, gnawing on lump of maple sugar. 'That is the Mighty One who cannot be conquered,' woman tells Glooskeb. 'That is Wasis. Meddle with him and there is trouble.'" Joe was rubbing his stump hand on his trouser leg again. Nell guessed it hurt him, but his voice betrayed no discomfort. Even the weariness seemed to dissolve. A lilt like singing came into his tone as he told the story of the Mighty One, the baby. "Glooskeb, chief of all living things, turned to baby with smile like morning sun and called him to him. Baby smiled but did not budge. Glooskeb made his voice like summer bird and called him to him. But Wasis sat where he was and sucked maple sugar. So Glooskeb frowned and spoke like thunder and ordered Wasis to come crawling to him. Mighty One, baby, began to howl. He stayed in same place."

Nell stood perfectly still. It seemed to her that no wall enclosed the dim little kitchen. She was where Joe was, with Louisa and Peter by the stove.

"Then," Joe finished, "Glooskeb had to sing the songs of power that call all things out of wood and rock and water and air. Glooskeb sang, and Wasis sat on ground listening with all his self. He liked that song very much, but he did not move. So Glooskeb gave up. Wasis sat on ground in sunshine, making baby sounds everyone think they understand. Few know baby gurgles and sings baby song because he remembers time he overcame Glooskeb, who conquered whole world. And still, from Old Time to new, baby alone not ruled by any master."

The stew, bubbling hard, flicked drops that leapt and sizzled as they spattered on the stove. Louisa said softly, "That's my best story of Glooskeb."

Released, Nell made her way with care out of the kitchen, past the table and chairs. She pulled the stew pot to the side of the stove.

"Will Mrs. Fowler's baby sing that song, too?" Louisa asked.

Nell glanced at Joe. She couldn't tell whether he nodded or whether he was shutting himself away again.

"Enough," Peter said to Louisa, but without his usual testiness. "Grandfather's said enough for now."

Louisa jumped up and went to the shelves. Soon she was setting out all the finery that Nell had just put away.

23/False Spring

During the night the wind veered to the south. In the morning the sky was milky and soft. Before their eyes, bare branches turned from silver to shiny black, with luminous drops suspended from every twig. The woods, silent for so long, sent forth a racket of jays and crows, squirrels and chipmunks, all frantic with hunger.

Louisa looked at Joe. "Is it spring?"

He shook his head. "False spring."

"January thaw," Peter put in.

Nell said, "How do you know it's January?"

"I'm guessing. Maybe it's February by now."

Melting ice dripped and pinged wherever it struck metal. Cakes of snow slid and thudded into the ground snow.

"If it stays warm for a while," Peter declared, "the tracks might be cleared. Then all we have to do is raise the engine and tender and go on by train."

Louisa turned a worried face to Joe. "If we do that, can we take Seesur and the moose?"

Peter groaned. "I was joking. Only a big crane can right the engine."

Nell decided it was time to get Louisa away from Peter for a while. "Let's go see if there's running water at the river."

They skirted the empty boxcar, standing aslant just below the palace car. Nell averted her eyes from the huge, snowy mounds beyond the hay boxcar. There was something awful about an enormous engine lying powerless under the snow. More of the wheels were already glinting through the melting cover.

But Louisa seemed to share Peter's fascination with the engine. Staring at it, she said, "Peter doesn't like me."

Nell could see the hurt and bewilderment in her eyes. She said, "He's just short-tempered because he can't do anything with the train."

They went on to the river. The ice jumble along the bank was thick, but farther out, water tumbled, drilling tunnels through the ice sheet. They tried to dislodge one chunk of ice to reach the water but only got themselves soaked and chilled.

Back in the warm palace car, their wet things in a heap beside the stove, Louisa said, "When we do go, we won't be this way anymore."

Nell fastened her dry skirt. "What way?"

"Like a family in its own house."

"This isn't a house, and we're not a family." It occurred to Nell that this might be a good time to tell Louisa about Joe.

Louisa's stockings had so many holes, it was hard for her to pull them on without ripping them even more. "Peter's getting to be an almost-brother to you," Louisa replied, yanking at her stocking. "I don't know how . . . how to have a brother."

"It doesn't matter," Nell told her.

"It does." Louisa's heel burst through the stocking. "I have Joe, don't I?"

"About Joe . . ." Nell began. "You oughtn't to think of him as—" She stopped short before saying *Grandfather* and finished with "Glooskeb."

But Louisa was so full of what she was speaking of that she wasn't listening. "Not just Joe," she went on. "I have the moose, too. He's my almost-brother. If we call him Brother Moose, then he'll be family, too."

Nell couldn't help laughing. She told Louisa that Brother Moose sounded just right. She realized that she couldn't shatter Louisa's notion of her family when they still didn't know whether

‡

the Fowlers would accept her or turn her away. But Louisa did need to be reminded that the palace car was only a way station for them. They were stalled here, that was all. Soon they would be on their way again.

But that evening Joe put a damper on Nell's hopes, telling them that if the thaw continued, the bobsleigh would bog down. "Still," he went on, "this is moon of crust on snow. Snow will come again with cold." He narrowed his eyes as though looking into the distance—or was it the future? "Maybe tomorrow moose go to work."

"The moose?" exclaimed Peter. "How?"

"Moose easy now. Can learn like horse. You see."

"He does what he likes," Peter maintained.

"Soon he like what we like. Pull tree first, then help him horse pull sleigh."

"Seesur and Brother," Louisa declared. "Brother Moose."

Peter burst out laughing. Even Joe smiled at the name. He said to Louisa, "Moose good brother, you think?"

"Oh, yes," she told him. "But he can't learn all at once. You'll have to be patient with him."

Joe nodded. "Tomorrow we show him, eh?"

Louisa beamed. "I wish we could start now. If only it wasn't dark. It's always night when we're not even sleepy."

"Days coming longer," Joe said, "like bird's footsteps, one at a time. Can't be hurried. I be patient with moose, you be patient with season."

"All right," Louisa agreed. She looked so happy, so sure.

Nell wondered what Peter thought of all this, but he had his face buried in the *Transcontinental Magazine,* touching one word after another with his finger. Those printed words he puzzled over were like bird's footsteps, too. It seemed as though everyone had to practice patience of one kind or another.

The thaw continued, thrilling and treacherous. The river changed constantly, swelling and spreading, freezing overnight, its contours shifting with each new sunset. They had fish again, and partridge and rabbit. Nell and Louisa, constantly wet, were chapped and raw.

Now that Joe was working with the moose, the animals were given their hay in the early morning to lure them back from their nighttime browsing. The moose didn't seem to mind his makeshift harness, but he was leery of the shafts when Joe detached the whiffletree from the sleigh and backed the moose between them. Eventually he found that he could lean to one side and scratch himself against the tip of one shaft. Groaning with pleasure, he rolled back his bulbous upper lip and accepted the shafts as well.

After Joe acquainted the moose with Seesur's collar, it was time to make one for the moose.

"Horsehair stuffing," Joe observed with satisfaction as he severed a leather arm from the easy chair. But he had to fashion wooden hames and reshape the chair arms. Louisa held them steady while he punched new holes for restitching. Nell, terrified that the chair would cost more than Joe could afford, dutifully wrote it down on the list.

Louisa held the moose's head while Joe measured and fitted the homemade harness. She learned to lead him without getting stepped on. Soon the moose was hauling a tree on the trampled snow. He was ready for the sleigh, ready to be hitched up behind Seesur. Joe lashed two trimmed pines to the shafts, but that made them too rigid. So he devised a second whiffletree, using chains from the tender and every available rope. Since the reins weren't long enough now, Peter had to ride Seesur.

Louisa couldn't bear being left out of the excitement. She trailed after Joe, confronting him at every turn, until he finally gave in and boosted her up onto the moose's back.

"Look at me!" she shouted to Nell, who was hanging out the wash on the platform rail.

But they didn't get very far before the runners bogged down in the soft snow.

Each morning Nell hurried out to see if winter had returned. But the air stayed springlike, and the baffled birds sought nonexistent seeds and grew tame with hunger.

"If we're so close," Nell finally blurted, "why don't we just walk and come back for the sleigh later?"

"Can't carry enough," Joe replied as he caught a length of rawhide in his teeth and cut it neatly with his good hand. He was using hair from Seesur's tail for thread now; it was glossy and strong.

"Nell's right," Peter argued. "We can hitch the horse to the whiffletree and drag on it what we need."

"I bring cradle," Joe responded. "I bring child and corn."

"The cornmeal's almost gone," Nell reminded him.

Louisa, practicing braiding velvet drapery cords, said, "You two need to learn patience like Joe and me."

Peter stalked out, slamming the door behind him.

Louisa dropped the braid and had to start all over.

"Let me show you," Nell offered. "You almost got it right."

It felt good to help Louisa again. These days she was too busy with real tasks for Joe to bother playing with the dining service. But even as she learned to keep pressure on the braid strands, her fingers kept fumbling with them. Nell stopped her when she lost track of one again. Louisa flared up.

"You don't want me to get it right."

"I do. I'm showing you. Look, you left this one out."

Louisa flung aside the cords and went to watch Joe, whose stump hand pressed the collar to his chest so he could cut through the stiff leather. Suddenly the knife snapped, the tip of the blade embedding itself in the leather. The rest of the blade, still attached to the hilt, flipped onto the carpet. Hissing, Joe retrieved the broken knife and gazed at it bleakly.

"There are kitchen knives," Nell said to him. "I can write one on the list if you like."

But Louisa had another plan. Clambering into the upper berth, she rummaged in the satchel. She returned to Joe, bearing the knife she had found in the woods. Nell could see at once that it was better for Joe, not because of the hilt shaped like a hand but because it was angled much like Joe's knife.

Joe turned it over and over on his knee, then rubbed the rusted blade. After that he rested his stump on the hilt-hand. Louisa stood directly facing him, her cheeks flushed with pride. It crossed Nell's mind that Joe and Brother Moose might be all Louisa could handle at one time. Two strands, then, not three.

Peter burst into the car with important news. Some of the tracks were exposed. He had been kicking at the snow along the line when great chunks of it had parted from the rails.

"I found the section that's out," he told them. "It doesn't look too bad. I think we can straighten it."

At first Nell couldn't understand why he wanted to bother with the dislodged track. But she could tell that he had an idea. He had been thinking so hard about it that it tumbled out backward.

"We don't need an engine," he blurted. "The horse and moose can pull this car."

Joe went to look over the tracks with him. The sun, assisted by the iron, had done its work.

"But railroad car great, heavy thing," Joe remarked doubtfully.

"It's different on tracks. The wheels roll on them."

Joe frowned. He walked around the car. Nell could hear Peter's rush of excitement and Joe's low, brief comments. Back at the place where the train had jumped the tracks, Joe kicked the cross ties and ballast under the snow. Nell could see that he was beginning to believe Peter.

"That means we'll still have our palace," Louisa declared.

Nell refrained from pointing out that if they could get the car rolling, they would soon arrive at its depot, where they would have to leave it. To give Louisa something to do while Peter and Joe were deep in talk, Nell said, "We'll have to give the car a good cleaning before we go."

Louisa jumped to the ground. "You clean." Already she was scrambling to catch up with them. "Joe will want me working with him," she threw back at Nell.

24/At Odds

Suddenly all their concern about the weather was reversed. Now they hoped for the thaw to hold. They were racing against time, against the winter that was bound to return. The girls kept busy hacking at the riverbank and dragging chunks of frozen sand to spread along the track. When the sand melted, it would be sprinkled on the rails to give the wheels enough traction to start them rolling. Peter had found a railroad tool, a long iron spike with a prong at one end. Joe dug that prong under the dislodged rail. He knew just where to block it, where to place the chain around the slanting spike, and how to position Seesur to pull the chain. He also cleared the area. If the chain slipped and the lever-spike gave way too soon, it would go hurtling into the air with tremendous force.

Peter, craning to take in every detail, said, "I never thought Grandfather could do something like this."

"Joe can do anything," Louisa replied.

Peter set his face, trying to ignore her. Nell could feel irritation stirring in her, too.

Seesur strained against the drag. Joe had to urge him forward. Then all at once the rail moved.

"Stop!" shouted Peter. "I think that's far enough." He ran to inspect the joint.

"Get back!" Joe yelled at him.

Scowling, Peter obeyed. Joe backed Seesur very slowly until the tension was gone from the drag and the chain slid down the spike. Only then did Joe approach the rail to examine it.

"This thing can go like shot," Joe said to Peter. "Like logs on river." He seized Peter by the shoulders, forcing Peter to meet his eyes. "Tomah had not enough fear. You learn it, learn fear."

Nell couldn't hear Peter's reply, but she saw Joe's arm reach around him before they separated. Louisa saw, too, and started to join them. Nell managed to catch hold of her sleeve.

"I go to Joe," Louisa protested.

She was even talking like him now. "You'll be in the way," Nell told her.

"Joe never thinks I'm in the way," Louisa flashed.

"Come on," Nell responded. "Joe needs us to get sand." But as soon as they were out of earshot, she tried to explain to Louisa that grandfather and grandson might want to be alone together for a while.

"He's my almost-grandfather, too," Louisa retorted.

Nell shook her head. "Not really."

"You just don't want me to have him," Louisa shot back. "You want me all for yourself. Or you want him."

"Him!" Nell swept on to the river, leaving Louisa standing by the hay boxcar, where the moose stood nudging the board that kept him from the hay. "You'd better feed Brother Moose," Nell flung back over her shoulder. "You're better off with him as family than Joe Pennowit."

"What do you mean?" Louisa cried.

Nell stopped and turned. "Because . . . because . . ." Her voice shook. She knew she ought to shut her mouth, but Louisa's face showed such stubborn righteousness that all Nell could do was lash out. "Because he's done the worst sin of all. He killed someone."

"Killed someone?" The color drained from Louisa's face.

"Yes."

"I don't believe you."

"It's true. One of those men in the woods. He told me himself."

"Told you himself?"

"Stop saying everything *I* say."

Louisa drew a breath. "It doesn't have anything to do with us. It can't. He's been good to us."

"I know he has. To prove to Mrs. Fowler that those neighbors, the Cartwrights, were wrong about him. He needs us the way he needs the moose." Even as she said this, Nell suspected she was being unfair to Joe just to get back at Louisa.

Louisa shook her head wildly, the curls bouncing like a mop. When she stopped, her eyes were full of misery and confusion. "What will happen to him?" she whispered. "What will happen to us?"

"I don't know. I didn't want to tell you. I don't understand all of it. I know he's been good to us, Louisa." Nell reminded her gently that Brother Moose was waiting for his hay. "You can put some out for Seesur, too. But be sure to tie Brother Moose so he doesn't eat both portions before Seesur comes back."

Louisa nodded. Shoving at the moose with her whole body, she pushed up the board and shimmied into the boxcar.

Nell went onto the river to wrestle with the frozen muck. Her insides felt like the chunks she grappled with, unwieldy lumps of sandy mud and stones and blackened leaves and sticks all churned together. Were the old feelings about Joe breaking up, too? Now that she could see him driven by revenge and fury, she felt less bound to the murder. Did that change anything, really? She couldn't tell.

After Peter put Seesur away, he spent the remainder of the day working with Joe on the rail. They evened the bed and wedged the tie securely in place. Their voices came and went as they puzzled out each step. At dusk they came in for their first meal of the day. They were worn-out and filthy, but satisfied. Nell gave them rabbit broth thickened with cornmeal. When they finished it, they drank quantities of water. It had been a thirst-making day.

Nell went to refill the water pail. At the riverbank, the moose suddenly loomed, huge and tranquil, something dangling and dripping from his mouth. Louisa must have forgotten to tie him.

Nell cupped her hands as if she were offering him a treat. Chewing slowly, the moose ambled over to her and lowered his bulbous muzzle. She felt his hot breath, his cool tongue. All she could do was reach for the hairy skin flap under his throat. "Come," she pleaded, but the moose planted himself firmly in the muck. "Come," she begged, "I'm your friend, too." But her voice rang false, false as this thaw, this unreal spring.

As the moose lurched away, she cried out, half in alarm, half in despair. Seesur, tied to a tree beside the boxcar, neighed. The moose gave an answering grunt. Seesur called more shrilly. Pretending not to care about the moose, Nell set off toward Seesur. She didn't have to look back to tell that the moose was following.

She used the empty pail to lure the moose. She hated playing such a mean trick on Seesur, who was sure there was feed in it, too, but she could think of no other way to keep the moose coming. It worked. The moose nearly knocked Nell over to push his way in with Seesur, who tongued the bottom of the pail even though it contained no cornmeal.

All Nell could do was unhitch Seesur and put his rope around the moose's neck. Leaving him tied to Seesur's tree, she scrambled up to the car platform, calling to Louisa.

Louisa was no more inclined to listen to her than the moose had been.

"Brother Moose needs you," Nell insisted.

With a sigh, Louisa came out. She had no trouble finding the moose halter in the dark. She had no trouble getting him to lower his head for her so that she could slip it on.

Nell minded that she hadn't been able to manage the moose entirely on her own. Louisa didn't even seem to notice that Nell had caught him before he wandered off too far. Louisa only remarked that they were lucky he was still here, since Joe intended for them to leave first thing tomorrow morning. Nell felt like telling her that more than luck was involved, but she knew it would be pointless. Now that the moose was safely hitched, Louisa didn't worry about having neglected to tie him to his tree in the first place. She seemed to be able to put anything from her mind that might have troubling consequences. Probably she had already dealt with the murder that way.

Nell tried to imagine what it would feel like to let go of thoughts so easily. What a relief it would be, like turning to someone else to decide what was right and what wrong, someone in charge and civilized and grown-up like Mrs. Fowler.

25/By Train at Last

Louisa, breathless with excitement and with the effort of slogging through the snow and mud, came wallowing to Nell with a message from Joe, who was getting the moose harnessed. Nell was to write a note on another sheet of paper in case anyone came along before they returned for the bobsleigh. Joe wanted to make it clear that the sleigh wasn't abandoned.

Nell sat at the desk and wrote in big block letters: PROPERTY OF MR. AND MRS. GABRIEL FOWLER. She took it to Joe, who was trying to back the moose between the shafts. Either the moose sensed the tension or he resisted, because he was being hurried. Louisa crooned and coaxed. She had a way with him, but still he laid his ears back.

"What did you write?" Joe asked Nell while he looped a strap through a chain link and drew it tight.

Nell read the message.

"Put down Macomber. Say, 'Jessie Macomber Fowler.' That name more likely known around here. Then put message on seat with stone on top."

By the time Nell returned from the sleigh, Seesur was in place ahead of the moose. That seemed to reassure the moose. Joe and Peter went to the rear of the palace car to get it ready for the start. While Louisa remained at Brother Moose's head, Nell stood beside Seesur. He lowered his head and blew softly into her hair. She sank her fingers into the soft place between his forelegs. His winter coat was long and lustrous.

"Why don't you come and pat Brother Moose?" Louisa invited.

"You have him quiet now. I'd only upset him."

"You like Seesur better than Brother Moose," Louisa said.

Nell could feel a Peter-like retort rising up in her. "Don't be silly" was all she said, adding almost grudgingly, "I'm still a little bit afraid of him."

Louisa didn't speak for a moment. Then she said, "His fur isn't as nice as Seesur's. He's not beautiful."

Nell left Seesur and came to look at Brother Moose, then at Louisa, who stood under his head rubbing his chest, too. His collar still looked to Nell like chair arms. "Yes, he is," Nell told Louisa with a smile. "With you there, he is."

Louisa grinned back at her. For an instant they seemed like the sisters they almost had been. But Nell couldn't help feeling a kind of sadness for what they had lost and were still losing.

Peter called them to the platform. Joe was worried about using the lever. If he or Peter were thrown backward, it might be hard to catch up to the car.

"We could just stop and wait," Louisa said.

"That wouldn't get us very far," Peter snapped.

Nell tried to explain to Louisa that the problem was getting the wheels to start. Once they got rolling, the car mustn't be allowed to slow down. If it stopped, Peter and Joe would have to begin with the lever all over again.

When they were all on the platform, Joe took the reins and flicked them hard. The moose plunged and staggered. Seesur leaned forward to pull. All Nell could feel was a faint jolt. Then the moose went berserk trying to break free. Joe and Louisa ran to him, Joe whacking his shoulder, Louisa plying him with loving words. No sooner was the moose calm than Seesur swung his rump and pawed.

"Careful," Peter shouted. "He'll shift those ties."

They had to brush pebbles off the rails and then sand them again. Now Joe was more concerned about managing Seesur. Even though the reins had rope extensions, Seesur was too far ahead to keep in perfect line, and there was always the danger that the long reins might catch in the moose's harness.

Peter thought he could ride Seesur and control him directly. But Peter was needed at the rear of the car, to get it started.

"I can stay on Seesur's back," Nell offered.

At first Joe wouldn't consider it, but eventually he had to agree. It was the only way.

When he boosted her up on Seesur, she did a lot of squirming, trying to arrange her skirt to protect her legs.

"Better get comfortable," Peter said. "You could be there a long time."

But where could she straddle the broad back without something jabbing her? She was still trying to pad her legs and backside when Peter's shout reached her from the rear of the car. "Ready?"

"Ready!" she lied.

"Ready!" Louisa echoed, all alone on the platform.

Then came a sound from another world, a squeal of iron wheels turning. Nell leaned back to whack Seesur's rump. He lurched, nearly tossing her from his back. While she clung to the harness turrets and pulled herself upright again, he strode forward.

Peter yelled, "Are you all right?"

Clutching the harness saddle in one hand, she swiveled enough to get a look at the moose stepping, heavy-footed but sure, between the cross ties. There behind him on the platform stood Peter and Louisa. "I think so," she called back. "Where's your grandfather?"

"Coming through from the other end of the car!" Peter shouted to her.

Settling herself as best she could, Nell faced forward. For a while she leaned way over so that she could grip the hames, but Seesur's long black mane kept whipping her face and making her eyes water. It was important to watch the roadbed ahead, even though Seesur was in his stride now and pounding right along between the rails.

Nell's heart was pounding, too. And then, before long, not just her heart but her whole body. Every time Seesur struck a cross tie, the jarring came straight up through him into her and rattled her teeth. She tried sitting straight, with her knees drawn up, but that felt like being perched on top of Wind-Blower. Lying flat was no good, either, with all those hard things digging at her.

When Seesur finally slowed, she was so grateful she just slumped down on him. Peter's shouts roused her from her trance. "Hit him! Keep him moving!"

It dawned on her that Seesur had slowed because they were going up a long rise. She gave Seesur a halfhearted whack. He was leaning into the climb and puffing hard. Turning, she stared at the moose, his ears going back and forth, his jutting shoulders like sluggish pistons. Every once in a while he thrust his bulbous nose toward Seesur's hocks, causing the horse to lunge forward. Then both animals settled into the climb, each pulling.

Now that the ride was slower and smoother, Nell tried to set herself to rights. She brushed back her hair and yanked down her skirt on either side.

"Look, look!" Peter called to her.

She couldn't hear the rest of what he was trying to tell her. There was so much clatter: harness hardware and chains jangling, the palace car rumbling behind. What did he want her to see? Peering to one side, she saw the usual trees. Peering the other way, she noted a difference, at first bewildering. Then, with stomach-wrenching clarity, she looked ahead and down, straight down into a chasm. Below her, below the trestle that bridged this gap, she saw what was either a narrowed river or a branch of it, set deep in rocky banks.

Clinging to the harness, she shut her eyes and pressed her face into Seesur's warm back. She waited a long moment after the sound of hooves on wooden planks was replaced by the solid thud she had been hearing before they'd crossed the bridge. Even after she opened her eyes, she had trouble looking at her surroundings. Still flattened against the horse, she glimpsed trees here, trees there. Finally she raised herself up to be sure. Now she dared to look back, but the palace car blocked her view of where they had been.

"Are we almost there?" she yelled at Peter.

"Don't know. Doesn't look like it."

"Will we stop to rest?"

"No."

"What if I fall off?"

"Don't." Then he added, "Were you scared?"

"Scared?" She only muttered this to herself. Never again, she promised. Never, ever again. "I shouldn't be here," she complained aloud to the green spruce tips bristling through the slush. With the track leveled off, the pulling was easier for the animals, though harder on Nell. Every time the horse or the moose was yanked by the different pace of the other, Nell was shaken. "It's not my fault," Nell told a red squirrel that dashed across Seesur's path and stopped to chitter at them. With a flick of its tail it darted away.

The river flowed into a pond. Nell glimpsed a long heap of logs and sticks, a beaver dam. Water tumbled out of sight, changed direction, and rejoined a stream that trickled below the dam. Now it was a river again, white with its snowy cap of ice, black where the water broke free along the shore. The woods went on unendingly.

Nell thought about falling off, not with fear but with desire. Think of lying on the ground. Closing her eyes, she saw pictures inside her lids. Then suddenly, guiltily, she remembered that she was supposed to be watching out for obstacles on the track. But Seesur's mane and her own hair and eyelids veiled what she could see of the rail bed. It helped to turn aside, to notice something new, even if it was an alder swamp, even if it was nothing more than a great boulder like a crouching giant clothed in furry black moss.

When a clanging came to her ears, she knew it had something to do with the palace car. She hoped for trouble that would force them to stop. At this point she didn't care if they never got started again. She would gladly walk back along the track to the sleigh. She would gladly wait for snow. She would do anything, anything to be still and down and finished.

Hoots and yells accompanied the clanging and forced her to straighten. Staring straight ahead, she saw dream structures. Pictures on the inside of her eyelids? But they weren't all run together. They were solid, squared. Buildings!

She needed Peter to confirm what she saw. Glancing back, she caught sight of Louisa on the platform banging a ladle against a copper kettle. Peter was hollering and waving like a madman.

As the tracks curved, the settlement revealed itself. There was a road that forked and then seemed to disappear under snow. It looked to Nell as though it was heading toward a three-story brick structure with tall smokestacks and some sort of scaffolding with a bridge high off the ground. Between that structure and the track there was open space and a row of frame sheds, houses, and a store, and one larger building with ANSASKEK HOTEL painted in bold letters across its front.

Nell fastened her gaze on the items advertised on the outside of the store: PROVISIONS, FANCY GOODS, FISHING TACKLE, CANOES. She read the words as though they were food and she was starving, gobbling without tasting, without taking in the emptiness of the place. Not a soul in front of the store, not a sound from the brick structure, not even a chicken or a dog in the mud and trampled snow.

The tracks petered out at a crudely roofed siding with not so much as a shed beside it for selling tickets.

"I'm braking!" Peter shouted.

Nell thought, So am I. Breaking. Broken.

"Haul in!" he yelled at the top of his lungs.

Nell grabbed reins and mane in her fists and had to let go and try again. Seesur gave a great sigh and stopped. Nell, still clutching the reins, saw two men emerge from the hotel, one in a frock coat running toward her, the other limping awkwardly with the aid of a stick. Both men were gaping at the sight of the palace car, pulled by moose and horse.

Peter walked right past Seesur and Nell, on his way to meet the men. Joe, following, held back. The men and Peter were suddenly talking, their voices jumbled as they reached Nell. She wondered how to arrange herself for sliding down. Her legs wouldn't unbend. All she could do was lean way over and swivel on her stomach to bring her legs together on one side.

"Wait!" one of the men shouted. "Stay there. My Tourograph!"

Was he speaking to Nell? What was a Tourograph? His voice rang like the kettle Louisa had banged. Nell could feel her skirt pull up. It was too late to stop her descent. She hoped to land on her feet, but her legs refused to support her.

Joe lifted her out of Seesur's way and was holding her in his arms when Peter and the frock-coated man ran to them. Nell looked straight at Peter. She felt perfectly clearheaded. All she had to do was explain that her legs were out of sorts. But when she tried to get the words out, her mouth went dry and her eyes oozed tears.

"What's wrong with you?" Peter demanded. He sounded cross and a little frightened.

Nell shook her head. Nothing, she wanted to tell him. She could feel Joe's stump hand between her shoulder blades. For once it didn't horrify her. She leaned back against him as he carried her to the hotel.

There was a pillow under her head. She looked up at a circle of gaslit lamps and wondered why they were on before dark. Closing her eyes, she listened to the voices swimming in and out of earshot, Joe's measured questions, Peter's rapid speech, and the unfamiliar voices in the accents of gentlemen. How good they sounded. Imagine noticing at a time like this that the men were well-spoken.

26/Ansaskek

This hotel looked little like the one where Nell had asked about train and stage connections. Its furnishings were plainer, its floors bare, except for a rug in front of the large fireplace in the dining area. After the ornate luxury of the palace car it felt a little strange and raw.

Other things felt strange, too. There was something uncanny in the clarity of the voices that came and went. It took a while for Nell to realize that there were no background sounds, no wagons rumbling or wheelbarrows crunching. Then another absence struck her: There were no women's voices here.

Rolling sideways, she tried to sit up. But she was so bruised and stiff, she couldn't hold back a cry of pain. She was just placing her feet on the floor when Louisa burst through the doorway and ran to her.

"Don't get up. You don't have to yet. Joe says."

Nell groaned. "I'm all right. Who are these people? Where are we?"

"It used to be an ironworks. Now it's being turned into a hotel. These men are from the train wreck. They stayed on purpose. Well, one of them couldn't walk. The others took the horses to get the engineer and fireman back, because they were hurt."

Both the man in the frock coat and the limping man came through. Louisa fell silent. The man in the frock coat introduced himself as Mr. Hargrove, assistant to the director of the company. Nell gathered that he was an important gentleman.

Mr. Hargrove nodded to his companion, the man with the bandaged leg. "This is Mr. Steele. We are in charge of the party here."

Nell was at a loss for words. A party in this place?

Peter came in to ask about feed for the animals. Mr. Hargrove said that all the hay had been left in the boxcar.

"Then I'll just hobble them for now, to let them browse," Peter decided. "They've worked up an appetite."

"Well, now," Mr. Hargrove put in. "So have we. There's been no meat since we ran out of ammunition. If you don't need the moose any longer, our young sporters would be delighted to have a shot at him."

"Hold on!" Mr. Steele said to them. "I'd like to get a picture of him first, with the horse and the child and the car, just the way they looked coming into Ansaskek. I'll get Freddy to set up my Tourograph—"

"You leave Brother Moose alone!" Louisa blurted. "Joe will get meat."

Mr. Hargrove regarded Louisa's flushed face and wild yellow hair with distaste. He exchanged a look with Mr. Steele. Then both men strode from the room.

As soon as they were out of earshot, Peter turned on Louisa. "Can't you keep quiet? Let Joe work out what's to be done."

Louisa glared back at him, then stomped out of the hotel.

"She was just trying to save the moose," Nell said.

"She doesn't understand. We're stuck with these people. It's their railroad car we've been living in. They brought a group of businessmen out here to get backers for turning the ironworks into a sportsmen's camp for city people who like to hunt and fish. They've been expecting someone to come to take them back. They've had enough of roughing it."

"Are they upset about the palace car?"

"They haven't been inside it yet. All they want right now is food. Joe made cornmeal mush for them. They had a lot of canned food to start with, but it's all gone."

Nell sighed. It occurred to her that they had come the wrong way. "Did Joe have any idea we'd end up here?" she asked Peter.

He shook his head. "It's confusing. This branch line is fairly new. Grandfather thought it was the main line going east. But it kept turning north. If we'd gone west from the wreck, the track would have veered south and connected with the main line. You go east on that line to get to Pawnook Carry, then take the road to Pawnook." He stopped. His voice dropped. "If we'd gone that way . . ." His words trailed off.

"You mean, all this time at the wreck we were practically there?"

Peter nodded glumly. "The train was only a day and a half out of Bangor. It came through Pawnook Carry just before the branch line. If we had gone the other way, we'd have reached the main line by now."

Nell tried to tell herself that it didn't matter. They were only a few days away from Mrs. Fowler now. Probably those men would come along in the palace car. Someone else could ride Seesur this time. "I want to look around," she said.

After Peter helped her out to the porch he went to look for his grandfather. "Don't forget about Seesur and the moose," Nell called after him. She gazed uphill at the massive brick structure, with its tall stacks and its bridgelike extension. Everything looked unreal, like a giant's playthings. Four men she hadn't seen before came toward the hotel and were joined by Mr. Hargrove and Mr. Steele. They all converged at the hotel porch, all exclaiming and jabbering about the extraordinary arrival of the palace car.

Peter came back and had to wait for a lull before he could tell them that Joe had gone out hunting. Nell could tell that he felt uncomfortable with these men, even though the four were much younger and more outgoing. Nell shared his uneasiness about them. They were too loud, too sure; they laughed as they spoke, and slapped one another on the back. Listening to them, it was hard for Nell to know how much they enjoyed being stranded in Ansaskek Village and how dearly they missed the comforts of home. When she asked one of them why they hadn't just followed the tracks back to civilization, he mentioned Mr. Steele's injured leg and the deep snow and bitter cold. There hadn't been enough snowshoes to go around, either. And by the time the thaw came, no one wanted to be far from Ansaskek, as they were certain rescuers would arrive momentarily.

The younger men followed her inside and showed her the way to the kitchen. One of them, who wore spectacles that gave him an owlish look, asked her to tell him about the Indian.

"You can ask him anything you want to know," Nell said. She opened the stove and looked around for wood. The kitchen was ample but also plain.

Another of the young men said, "The trouble is, Indians tell you what they think you want to hear."

Nell didn't think it was necessary to respond. She didn't know Indians, only Joe.

The young man went on to say, "It's part of Indian nature to be devious."

"They make the best guides, though," said one of the others.

"Maybe so, but you have to watch them. My guidebook says never pay up till you're ready to part with them, or they're likely to leave you high and dry."

"Joe wouldn't do that," Nell declared hotly.

"Oh, maybe not yours. He seems a fine fellow. I wish I'd known he was going hunting."

The owlish young man who had asked Nell about Joe said he was interested in Indian lore. So she talked to him while she fired up the stove and started water heating in a big pot. As she spoke of spruce shelters and moccasins, the birch-bark moose call, and the hooded jacket, the other young men wandered off. The owlish one took her to the cellar and helped her scratch through crates of sand for potatoes and onions and parsnips. By the time she had a broth simmering with the rubbery remnants of sprouting vegetables, she was all talked out. When he left her in the steamy kitchen, there remained only the slightest prickle of misgiving at the edge of her sagging thoughts.

Louisa, sobbing wildly, broke into Nell's peaceful solitude. Nell had to wrench Louisa's arms apart to keep her from clutching herself in the old, bobbing way. Nell finally plunged the hem of her skirt in a basin of water and slapped it over Louisa's head. Louisa gasped. Her sobs turned to quick, scratchy sighs.

Nell peeled back her skirt and drew Louisa over to the bench against the wall. "No crying," she commanded. "Just say what's wrong."

Louisa, still distraught, babbled, "Not his fault. It isn't. He didn't know it's the last. Poor Brother Moose. He's hungry, that's all."

Gently but firmly, Nell pried more out of Louisa. "He ate fringe? Tassels?"

Louisa shook her head. "Cornmeal. It was just left there, open." She heaved a jagged sigh. "What will they do to him?"

"Is any left?"

Louisa dragged her sleeve across her eyes and wiped her nose. She shook her head. "I know Peter will tell."

"We'll ask him not to."

"He will. And they'll kill Brother Moose."

"They won't, Louisa. Joe's bringing meat."

"Brother Moose has such a big appetite. There's nothing for him to eat around here."

"He always finds something," Nell reminded her. "And shows Seesur."

"He showed Seesur the cornmeal."

"Oh." To mask her own concern, Nell said she was sure he would find those twigs he liked. "You know, the ones with the knobs on them."

Louisa shook her head. "It's too hard when he's hobbled. He can't step right."

Nell thought that was true. She sent Louisa out for the sack in case any leftover meal could be shaken or scraped from it. Later, when Peter came in, she mentioned the hungry animals. Maybe they should be allowed to go free, she said, to give them a chance to find decent food.

"They've done pretty well for themselves so far," he remarked.

"They worked hard today."

"So did we." Then he added, "All right. I'll take the hobbles off." Glancing through to the dining room, he lowered his voice. "I wish Grandfather would get back. These people . . . I don't know how to talk to them. They think being in the woods is fun. They yell at me as though they think I don't understand."

"Joe will be back soon. It's dark already."

"Yes, and it's started to snow."

After Peter left her to see to the animals, she spread her skirt over the back of a chair beside the stove. The steam from the pot and from the drying fabric lulled her. Then all of a sudden she was jolted awake by a clamor signaling Joe's arrival. Nell couldn't help noticing that some of the voices sounded disgruntled. She soon found out why. The carcasses of the muskrats and rabbits Joe brought looked a little skimpy with all those hungry men looming over them.

Joe said, "Maybe tomorrow I catch him caribou."

"Tomorrow," boomed Mr. Hargrove, "we should leave here. We'll all go back together."

Joe didn't reply. While Nell made rabbit stew, he roasted muskrat in the open fireplace. Louisa brought in all the cornmeal she could scrape off the ground, so there were bits of needles and twigs and acorn shells in it. Nell was beyond caring. It seemed a lifetime ago when she and Seesur had scrambled for acorns during her search for Louisa. She dumped Louisa's scrapings, already lumpy from the new snow, into the stew. She hoped she hadn't added any pebbles.

As she stirred the pot, she sipped some of the gravy, thickened with cornmeal. When she brought it into the dining room, Joe didn't join the men at the long table. Instead he crouched on the hearth over the roasted muskrat, eating from the blade of the hand-knife. One of the young men bringing his plate to Joe asked him whether he had carved the hilt. In reply Joe showed his fingerless hand.

"How did you lose your fingers?" the man asked.

"On river," Joe said. "In logjam."

Peter broke in with questions about the train accident. All at once they were talking about the derailment, about how astonishing it was that a little something frozen on the rail could cause such damage. It had happened in an instant, the locomotive jumping the track and pulling it out of line, the tender and one boxcar tumbling after it. Mr. Hargrove remarked on how fortunate they were that the boxcar carrying the horses didn't go over. The horses had made it possible to get the seriously injured out.

"And we assume," he added, "that they made it out in good order, and also got word to our families and businesses. It was the early blizzard that interfered with their getting back here, I'm sure. But I'm surprised it's taken them this long."

Mr. Steele asked Joe whether he would cut across the river and head due south from Ansaskek. He had a feeling this could be done by someone familiar with these woods.

Joe shook his head. "Not now. River not safe."

"But to follow the track," Mr. Hargrove objected, "it's so much longer."

Joe, sucking on a bone and then tossing it sizzling into the flames, only nodded.

"That's an Indian for you," one of the younger men muttered. "Time's nothing to them."

Peter, out of questions, jumped up to gather bowls and spoons from the table.

"We might want to do some hunting on our own," Mr. Hargrove pursued. "We have only a Winchester eight-shooter and a shotgun. I think you should leave some cartridges with us before you turn in for the night, and maybe another rifle."

Joe rose and walked to the door. Nell and Louisa wiped the

table and went into the kitchen to wash the dishes. Later, on their way out to the palace car, Nell saw a box of cartridges on the clean table. Since no one was in sight, she turned out the lamp on the mantelpiece.

The falling snow gave the empty village an eerie look. Nell's and Louisa's soft moccasins whispered through the fresh snow. They sounded like shuffling ghosts.

Nell was so stiff and sore, she had trouble climbing into the berth. Slipping off her skirt, she let it drop to the carpet. She thought about going down again to hang the skirt up to finish drying. Then she snuggled down under the covers and thought no more.

27/Thin Ice

I t was not yet light when Nell heard Joe beginning to stir. By the time Peter got up and followed him outside, Nell was wide awake and planning a big wash so they would all be presentable when they arrived in Pawnook. She had to move slowly at first; she was still stiff. Even pulling on her skirt was hard.

Louisa rolled over and yawned. "Is it morning?"

"Almost," Nell answered.

"Still snowing?"

Nell pulled aside a curtain. "I think so. Yes. Snow or mist. And it's lighter than I thought."

The words were scarcely out of her mouth when two rifle shots rang out in quick succession, followed by a third. Crows raked the silence that followed the shots.

Louisa yawned again. "Joe hunting already?"

Nell hesitated. He couldn't be. Not right here in Ansaskek Village. Something was wrong then. But what? Trying to sound offhand, she said to Louisa, "It could be one of those sporters shooting crows."

She pulled on her shawl and stepped out onto the platform. Through a dense haze she caught sight of figures running toward the hotel. Then others materialized. It was impossible to tell what they were up to. They seemed to spin, arms upraised and waving, faceless and spectral and silent. Someone shouted; she couldn't see where the shout came from, but someone closer relayed the call: "Bring ropes! And the Indian! Get the Indian!"

Skidding on the icy steps, Nell landed in new snow and started to run in the direction of the hotel. But the men were coming out of it, a straggling line of them pulling on jackets as they went, sleeves flapping, voices snagged in the baffle of mist and snow. So Nell turned, catching up with a few of them, with no idea of where they were heading. They crossed the siding and plunged down to the river. Some went on, some stopped to point.

"What is it?" she cried. "What's happened?" She peered out over the white ice sheet and the swift, black water. A dark mound seemed to rise up out of the river. Then it subsided, becoming one with the torrent that rushed between boulders. Just when she decided she had seen nothing, that her eyes had been tricked by the whiteness, the moose emerged among the rocks and logs, floundering to gain a foothold.

Just like him, Nell thought. Just like Brother Moose to cause a commotion at the break of day. Probably his greediness had brought him too far out and he had broken through the shell of river ice.

One young man seemed to be trying to pick his way out to him.

"Don't scare him," Nell shouted. "He doesn't know you."

The young man raised a rifle.

Mr. Steele called from the siding, "Save your cartridges. He's done for."

Nell whipped around to protest. She didn't know whom to speak to. Where were Joe and Peter? Where was Seesur?

Behind her, the owlish young man was muttering, "Fools! Stupid fools!"

Nell spun around again, trying not to lose sight of Brother Moose. She took heart from the way he seemed to be pulling himself up. For an instant he gained his full height. Then he pitched forward onto his knees. The foam swirling around him turned pink.

All Nell could think was that he had cut himself on the rocks. He was trapped by those terrible logs that rolled around and under him.

He flailed out, trying to heave himself free, only to go down once more. His huge mouth, cherry red, gaped as he struggled for air.

The man with the rifle had regained the solid bank. The owlish young man said to him, "What's one more shot? Put the animal out of its misery."

And the one with the rifle shook his head. "There's the Indian now. He'll see to it."

Joe was working his way along the bank from upstream. When he was just across from the moose, he stood poised for an instant before skimming across the ice canopy.

Nell was distracted by a new sound, a kind of humming. It came from Louisa, who stood close by now, her eyes fixed on Joe.

"Don't look," Nell tried to say to her. "Oh, don't look."

A curious growl rose from Louisa's throat.

When the other bystanders gasped, Nell swung back around to watch. Joe had vanished. There were murmurs along the bank, but mostly everyone was very quiet. Except for Louisa. Then Joe reappeared. Now he was behind the moose. Was he waving? No, he was raising up the knife, bringing it down. The water ran black; it spurted red.

Mr. Hargrove shouted to Joe, "Save it! Save the moose!"

That made no sense to Nell. How could Brother Moose be saved if he was dead?

From uphill, Mr. Steele picked up the call. "Save him! Save that meat!"

Someone was already trying to throw a rope to Joe. It took several tries before Joe caught the end and wound it around the moose. Already logs and slabs of ice, like shards from an enormous window, were shifting. As soon as someone had tied the land end of the rope to a tree, Joe hooked his arm over it to bring himself to shore.

Louisa lumbered out into the swirling shallows to meet him. He was wiping the dripping hair from his eyes when she lunged at him. Staggering, he grabbed one of her pounding fists.

"Don't!" Her voice cracked like splintered ice. "Don't touch me!" She kept on striking him with her free hand. "Killer! Murderer!"

Mr. Hargrove spoke out from up the bank. "See here, child. He didn't shoot the moose. He just—"

But no one else existed for Louisa, not even Nell, who tried to call her back. The others gathered there seemed embarrassed by Louisa's outburst. They spoke among themselves.

"Unfortunate turn of events."

"It was just out there. I assumed— It wasn't hobbled. I thought it was wild."

Mr. Hargrove's command rose above the voices. "Get the Indian to a fire. Dry clothes."

But Louisa still faced Joe and stood in his way. "It's what you do. You kill and kill, the way you killed that man. Now I know it's true. Give me the knife." Her words burst into a sudden, horrified silence.

Releasing Louisa's wrist, Joe pulled the knife from his belt and extended it toward her, hand first. Snatching it, she ducked past him and splashed out toward the moose, her whole body rolling from side to side. When she lost her footing, she grabbed for the rope and pulled herself on into deeper water. Then she was there, with the moose, scrambling on and over him with the knife in one hand. She had to saw at the rope to cut through it. Kneeling on the moose, she bent to the effort, both hands gripping the hand-hilt.

The taut rope twanged over the water to the tree where it was lashed. Then it went slack. Everyone shouted at once and started running along the bank as the moose, cut free, was carried downriver. Midstream, the moose rolled, his legs waving in the snowy air. Then they flopped sideways and vanished. A raft of logs released by all the churning nudged the animal on. Louisa, still clinging to the rope around his neck, went hurtling with him and the logs toward the rapids.

"Hurry!" Peter yelled. He was leading Seesur down to them from upriver.

"Everything's letting go!" Mr. Hargrove shouted.

Someone untied the rope from the tree, carried it downriver, and hurled it toward Louisa. She didn't even lift her hand to try to catch the end that slapped the water beside her. Instead, a moose leg rose from the bloody foam like a disembodied limb.

All at once the shouts died away. Joe was on the river again, this time treading logs, sending each one spinning as he moved to the next. At one moment he seemed headed straight for the rapids. At the next he sidestepped nimbly, his arms outspread. Where was Louisa? All Nell could see was Joe running in place on a rolling log. Then he stepped off it into a small gap of clear water.

Nell thought he had lost Louisa and was somehow confused, grabbing the moose by mistake. Then she saw Joe wrench Louisa's arm away from the rope around Brother Moose.

"He won't be able to hold her," gasped Peter, beside Nell now. "He needs two hands."

One of the logs struck something, rose straight into the air, and snapped like a matchstick. Someone cried out. Nell couldn't utter a sound.

Downriver, the men were throwing the rope again and again. All at once a cheer went up. Peter yanked Nell's arm and tried to drag her along with him. Her skirt snagged and ripped. "Wait!" she gasped, her moccasins slipping and sliding, the cold air seizing her throat.

By the time she made it to the bank above the rapids, one of the younger men was carrying Louisa out of the river, another untying the rope from around her waist. Her face was livid and scraped; she was spewing water. She didn't seem to see anyone or anything, but she still clutched the knife with the hand-hilt.

Others were throwing the rope yet again, but not at the moose. So where was Joe? Then Nell understood. Peter was creeping out over the ice canopy, or what remained of it this close to the rapids.

She wondered whether he could see Joe. She wondered whether Joe knew that Peter was coming. If the ice gave way and Peter was swept downriver, Joe would see him then. It would be his nightmare come true.

The rope slithered out over the ice within Peter's reach. Pausing to tie it around his waist, he crawled on. From beneath him, a black streak crazed through the ice and branched like a root sending forth a dozen finer veins. All at once, loud as a thunderclap, the ice shattered. A glassy sheet shot out of the water. Peter tumbled behind it. But he was practically there now. A tiny island between him and the moose blocked the logs, sending them into the main current away from the shore.

Joe could be seen in the open water. He seemed to be shouting at Peter, but the crashing current drowned out his voice. Peter swam first one way, then reversed himself. He and Joe came together while he handed over the rope he had carried around his waist. Joe made his way back to the moose, struggling to lash it tight, and the rope became an overhand bridge between the moose and the shore. It was impossible to tell whether Joe propelled Peter or Peter supported Joe. Maybe it was some of each, because they stuck together as they clung to the rope, until they reached the shallows and could splash ashore.

When Nell got to them, Peter was sitting with his knees drawn up, his body convulsed with shivers.

"Carry him," Nell ordered, and two young men gathered Peter up.

Joe crouched with his back against a tree. Nell placed her hands on his crossed arms. They felt like ice.

"Let me help you," she said to him.

He focused bloodshot eyes on her. She tried to pull him up, but he might as well have been frozen to the base of that tree.

"Joe," she pleaded.

"Tell them," he whispered. "Tell them moose tied. Won't hold long. Jam break, moose go."

"All right," she said. "But you have to get inside now."

"Tell them," he rasped.

"Yes, I will." Tell them what? she wondered. Was Joe just raving senselessly?

Clawing at the tree with his good hand, Joe lurched to his feet. "Tell them," he repeated, coughing and spitting and barely forming the words, "they pay for him moose." He was shaking so hard, he could barely stand. Nell understood that he shook from more than the cold; he shook because of Peter, like Tomah, at the head of the rapids.

Joe's icy stump dropped to Nell's shoulder. She could feel his terror in that blunt weight, all his rage.

"Settle account," he mumbled. Then he shuffled away, his feet dragging through the trampled snow, his shoulders hunched and sharp through his drenched clothes.

28/Settling Accounts

Nell was on her way to the palace car when she found Seesur, caught by his dragging halter rope. He gave his low, stuttery greeting as she bent down to release him. Then he thrust his muzzle upward and neighed. She knew he was calling the moose. All she could do was lean against his leg and flank, taking more comfort from his stolid warmth than she could give. She tied him firmly to the car before going in.

Joe's wet clothes, draped around the stove, gave off a familiar stench. Joe, wrapped in a blanket, was shoving things into an empty cornmeal sack.

Peter, huddled under another blanket, said bleakly, "He's going."

"Enough snow soon," Joe commented. "You take sleigh."

"You mean, we're leaving Mr. Hargrove and the others?"

"Their people coming for them. Plenty meat."

"He means," explained Peter, "he's leaving us. Heading west, into Vermont, then north."

"But—" Nell stopped at the sound of approaching voices.

Mr. Hargrove and Mr. Steele came through the narrow door into the car.

"That girl needs dry clothes," Mr. Hargrove said to Nell. "When you've taken care of her, we want to talk with you." He turned to Peter. "You, too." Only then did he look at Joe. "We must ask you to butcher the moose. Can you get it ashore?"

Joe pulled the blanket tighter. He nodded.

Looking up and down the car, Mr. Hargrove observed, "I see you've made yourself at home."

Nell spoke up. "Everything is in order, plates, glasses, everything."

Mr. Hargrove said, "Under the circumstances, I'd like this arrangement to end."

"Under the circumstances," Mr. Steele echoed, his gaze fixed on Joe, "we think you owe us an explanation. It's a shock to learn that there's a murderer in your midst."

Joe returned Mr. Steele's look.

"If you have nothing to say," Mr. Hargrove declared, "then we'll take these two along with us right now."

Nell expected Joe to object, but he seemed unconcerned, unconnected with Mr. Hargrove's business. Nell glanced at Peter, awkward in his blanket. He looked angry and bewildered all at once. She said, "I'll just get some warm things for Louisa."

"Do that," Mr. Steele told her. "Meanwhile we'll begin with this young man." He beckoned to Peter, who followed him out of the car.

Nell tried to draw a deep breath before turning to Joe. She had to keep her voice low in case any of the sporters were still within earshot. "You won't leave us? You never did, never would." Her throat tightened. "Peter's wrong. Tell me he's wrong."

Joe shook his head. "No other thing to do now they know."

How could she plead with him when he was running for his life? She tried to tell herself it was for the best, to remind herself it was exactly what she had wanted. But nothing she thought really penetrated. She still couldn't catch her breath, couldn't look at Joe without the sting of tears.

Snatching up some dry clothes, Nell left the palace car and went directly to Louisa, who was bundled in a quilt in front of the big fireplace. She still had all her wet clothes on underneath. Nell took her into the kitchen to get her changed into dry things. Louisa did nothing for herself, but she didn't resist Nell, either. Indifferently she twisted around to allow Nell to pull off her blouse. The knife clattered to the floor. Louisa spoke in a leaden voice. "I have no family anymore. My brother is dead."

Nell shoved Louisa's inert arm into the sleeve of the fur jacket. "Can't you ever think before you talk?" She felt as though Peter were speaking through her. "Joe has to go away now. Because you told on him. Because they all heard, they all know." Nell shoved Louisa down on the bench, picked up the knife, and slapped it onto her lap.

Louisa lowered her wounded eyes. "Know what?" she mumbled.

"Never mind." Nell could feel another Peter-like retort on the tip of her tongue. But what good would it do if Louisa didn't understand what she had done. "I'll be back," Nell said to her. "They want to talk to me in the other room."

She found Peter in a chair, still wrapped in the blanket, the men standing around him.

"That's all, really," Peter was saying. "I don't think I should be talking about it."

Mr. Steele spoke in a kindly way. "You won't harm your grandfather. You must know all of this has to come out."

Peter shook his head. "I only know—"

"What? What else do you know?"

"What Grandfather told me," Peter finished lamely. "The reasons. And what happened before."

"Circumstances can change the look of things. As they already have right here today."

Nell spoke from the doorway. "Joe's done nothing here but help you."

Turning, they regrouped, drawing her into the room and nodding Peter out of it.

"When you're older," Mr. Hargrove said to her, "you'll understand that a man can't feel the same toward a criminal. Of course we'll have to turn him in."

"He thought he'd be safe after he crossed the border from Canada."

"A crime is a crime wherever it takes place. Surely you know that."

Nell drew a long breath, willing herself not to cry, not to weaken before them. They didn't guess that Joe was planning to leave. Finally she managed to ask, "What will happen when you turn him in?"

They shook their heads. They couldn't say. "Indians have to face up to the fact that they can't be savages in this day and age."

"He's not a savage," Nell blurted, and the tears spilled over.

"What he did is savage," Mr. Hargrove responded. "Although," he added, "it doesn't sound as though he intended to kill the man. It would have been easy to stab him in his sleep. But, according to Peter, his grandfather was trying to make the fellow say what he had done with you."

Nell covered her face. In all the times she had thought about Joe and seen the terrible deed in her mind's eye, it had never crossed her mind that Joe might not have meant it to happen that way. Hadn't he, himself, declared that he had wanted to kill that man? Nell mumbled through the shield of her spread fingers. "All the time in the woods, all I could think of was getting back to civilization."

"You're safe now," Mr. Hargrove told her.

But Nell was no longer sure what being safe actually meant, or, for that matter, what civilization meant. Wiping her eyes and nose, she faced Mr. Hargrove. He was speaking of rules and law; Joe had spoken of the murder in his heart.

"The authorities may take into account that he didn't desert you to save himself," Mr. Steele offered.

Nell grasped at this. "Could you tell him that?" Here was a chance to keep Joe from running off and making things look worse for himself.

Mr. Steele replied, "The less said just now the better. We need that moose butchered."

Nell couldn't leave it at that. "Joe was hurt, too. They beat him when they took Seesur and me and the wagon."

"Caesar?"

"Our horse, Seesur. He's a very good horse."

Mr. Steele smiled at her. "A good horse with a noble name. I'm sorry I never got that photograph of him and the moose pulling the train, and you riding on top."

"Do you know about Seesur?" Nell asked him.

"I know about Julius Caesar, the Roman emperor," Mr. Steele told her. "Is that what you mean?"

Nell could feel the heat rising into her face. She had heard of Julius Caesar, too, but she had never thought of Seesur that way. To cover her embarrassment she said, "There's a little gravy left from the stew. I'll make it into a broth for Louisa and Peter and Joe."

They thought that was a good idea. They were finished with her for now. She was glad to get away to the kitchen.

While Nell waited for the stove to heat up, she dropped Louisa's clothes into a basin of cold water. Stirring the soiled blouse, shift, and skirt, it came to her that this blood could have been Louisa's. She had come so close to being swept away, along with the moose and the timber he'd dislodged. She might have been crushed or drowned like Tomah Pennowit.

Brown grime rose from the material as Nell plunged it up and down in the basin. Clear one moment, soiled the next, the water swirled like her thoughts, showing nothing. A little while ago she would have turned to Mr. Hargrove and Mr. Steele with relief. Now all she could think of was how best to protect Joe from these determined, law-abiding men. She supposed that made her a savage, too.

As soon as the broth began to simmer, she filled three mugs. One she placed in Louisa's bruised hands. Then she set off with the others to the palace car. But Joe had already left to hitch Seesur to the whiffletree. Seesur would have to skid the moose carcass out of the river, the way he used to skid logs for Gabe Fowler.

"Aren't you going to help him?" Nell asked Peter.

Peter blew across the steam rising from the mug. "He says he can do it without me."

Nell nodded. So Peter didn't have the stomach for it. "Then what?" she asked.

"Then I suppose he'll leave." Peter sent her a look. "I hope you know better than to tell Louisa." Nell ducked her head. "She'll only let it out," Peter said.

To cover her guilty start, Nell asked him whether they ought to try to change Joe's mind. That brought a wan smile to Peter's lips. Then he grew thoughtful. "After Grandfather goes, Louisa should stay in the hotel with those men."

"Oh, no," Nell protested. "We have to bring her back here. She's a part of us."

"Not anymore," Peter declared stiffly.

"She said something like that, too," Nell murmured. "That she has no family anymore."

Peter snorted, then drained the mug.

Taking it from him, Nell said, "We're the most family she ever had. Ever. I can almost imagine what it's like. I've tried and tried to remember my brother. For a long time, when I pictured him, all I could see was a boy I knew on the island. And now . . ." Her voice fell away.

"Now?" he prompted curtly.

She met his eyes. "Now I suppose it'll be you I see when I try to picture him. It's all I can do, even though I know he's real and that he came looking for me. But Louisa never had a brother, not that she knew of. So she could never even make one up. Until Brother Moose."

Peter looked away. Then, glancing at his grandfather's mug of broth, he said, "It's getting cold."

"I'll heat it again."

At the sound of voices outside, they went to the door together to find the young men gathered around Joe and all speaking at once. With an exclamation of annoyance one of them stalked off to the hotel. Within minutes Mr. Hargrove and Mr. Steele, clapping their hands and blowing on their fingers, followed the young man over to the group.

Mr. Hargrove started speaking to Joe. "I hear the horse is hitched and ready and you're balking. Holding out on us?"

"Settle first," Joe replied. "Nobody feel cheated after."

Mr. Hargrove agreed that was sound business practice. They could discuss the terms in the hotel, where it was warm.

"No," said Joe. "Here. Now."

"Then speak up before we all get frostbite."

"There is moose," said Joe, "with or without skin."

"The skin, by all means. It's the only trophy we'll have to show for all this."

"Meat for me," Joe added.

"Meat for all of us. We're in this together."

Joe shook his head.

Mr. Hargrove shrugged. "Help yourself. It doesn't matter. We'll have to leave most of it behind, anyway."

"You pay for him moose?"

"Agreed. What else?"

"Knives for skinning, for cutting. I choose."

Mr. Hargrove and Mr. Steele exchanged an uneasy glance. Nell could see that they didn't like the idea of handing over knives to a man who settled disputes with them. They might believe that circumstances could change the look of things, but they would not forget that he had set himself against them and dictated the terms of the moose payment.

Joe ignored the look that passed between them. He fixed his

gaze downriver where the logjam was, where the moose was, and the rapids, and where Seesur stood hitched and ready.

The men conferred briefly. Then they left to bring whatever sporting knives they had from the hotel.

"Money, too," Joe reminded them as they dispersed.

It took all the rest of the day to skin the moose and get some of the butchering done. Joe returned to the palace car after dark. He did not unhitch Seesur from the whiffletree, but left him restless and hungry outside the far end of the car.

"Are you taking Seesur?" Nell asked him.

"We go together," Joe said. "All together, I think."

"All of the men?" Peter exclaimed.

"All the way to Pawnook?" Nell asked eagerly.

Joe shook his head. "No men. Just us. Hard going on bridge, I think. So we go together awhile."

"What about Louisa?" Nell ventured.

Peter turned aside in irritation but didn't speak.

Joe shrugged. "You see." Then he added, "Maybe you see. Go in hotel now, make big meal in there so them men sleep well."

The men in the hotel seemed relieved to be rid of Joe. They talked more or less comfortably among themselves as they enjoyed the generous portions of moose steak Nell fried for them. Louisa sat clutching the hand-knife and rocking on the bench. Every once in a while a fit of coughing seized her; otherwise she was silent. As Nell came and went, she thought of comforting things to say, but they all clogged in her throat before she could get them out. Louisa went on rocking in her dumb misery.

Nell didn't wait to clear the table before hurrying back through the snow to the palace car. Joe had prepared moose steak, too. Nell thought she wouldn't be able to touch it, but this was different somehow, because she hadn't cooked it herself. Famished by now and telling herself it was just meat, she gobbled it down.

When the door opened and Louisa came in, they all went still, as if caught in some wrongdoing.

Louisa said, "I came away from that place because I didn't want to be with the smell."

"It's here, too," Nell warned her.

"Not as bad."

Joe speared a piece of the meat with the borrowed knife and put it in his mouth.

"I made trouble for you," Louisa said. "I heard them talking."

Joe swallowed before replying. "Joe make trouble for Joe." He speared another chunk of meat and held it out to her. "Eat," he said.

Louisa sat down, lumpy in the fur jacket. "I can't."

"You don't eat," he told her, "you die."

Louisa nodded. "I thought of that. Then I would find Brother Moose in heaven."

Joe grunted. "Long hunt, that one. In moose heaven no Louisa, only cow for young bull."

"Don't go," Louisa whispered.

Nell gasped. Louisa had understood her, after all.

Peter turned on Nell. "You told her?"

"I had to," she flashed at him.

Joe dragged his chair around to face Louisa. His voice low, he spoke of the first time he had called the moose and of not killing him. "Next time, this time, moose call me. Call me to kill."

"He was already dying," Louisa said thickly. A harsh cough was ripped from her throat. When it was over, she had barely enough breath to add, "I know that now."

Joe tapped his chest with his stump. "Kill him moose. Not hungry. Not angry. Kill him because he call, only for that. Kill your brother and mine."

His words settled over them like windless snow, filling all the pits and smoothing all the creases in the landscape of their life together, making whole what had been split and mauled. Louisa drew the hand-knife from inside the fur jacket and laid it on his knee beside his stump. Then she stood up, pulled off the jacket, and climbed up to her berth.

Joe instructed Nell to bring out the account sheet, to settle one last time. She read over each item. When she was finished, he gave her a wad of dollars for Jessie Fowler. It wasn't enough, but it was all he could manage for now. He told Peter that in another year he would be free to look for a railroad job. Only he must be sure the Fowlers had enough time to find someone to take his place.

"I thought we were going together to the sleigh," Peter objected. "You talk as though you're leaving us now."

"We are together to main train line, but this may be last quiet time before we go two different ways. At main line I head west. You follow tracks east to Pawnook Carry, then find road to Pawnook. Maybe two days for you. Long way for me." He looked at Nell. "Write on paper."

She found another half sheet in the desk drawer. Joe dictated: "To company of Ansaskek Ironworks. Plenty meat left. Account closed. I don't pay whole chair anymore because you kill moose, so moose collar no use. Now you have them chair arms back. We send help plenty time."

"Is that all?" Nell asked.

"What other thing to say?"

She stared at the letter. "You could add, 'Yours truly.'"

Joe shook his head. "No. Not theirs. Truly never theirs."

It struck her that he wasn't venting his anger anymore. He was simply rejecting what these men stood for and claiming his own heritage.

He bent over the half sheet to sign his name, the letters sprawled across the paper. He didn't ask whether they were correct but impaled the sheet with the borrowed knife to the inside of the door. He told everyone to get a few hours sleep. They would leave before light. It would be very cold.

Nell looked around at the mess. "Shouldn't we clean up? I haven't even washed the sheets."

Peter, shoving wood into the stove, burst out laughing. "And hang them out in the snow? That would be a pretty sight for the sporters in the hotel. They wouldn't have much trouble figuring we were up to something."

Nell remembered then that she had left Louisa's clothes hanging in the hotel kitchen. She would have to go and fetch them. The snow was coming down in earnest, tiny ice pellets stinging her face and hands as she ran from the siding to the hotel.

No one seemed surprised when she passed through into the kitchen. Then she realized they must think she had come back to wash the dirty dishes. For a moment she hesitated. The plates and cutlery were strewn every which way. She had to force herself to turn away from them. After she yanked Louisa's things from the line, she grabbed a handful of tea leaves and a few matches and rolled them inside Louisa's stockings.

On her way out of the kitchen she ran into the owlish young man, who was heading for the stairs. He gave her such a friendly smile that she was overcome with remorse and asked him if it was all right to take some matches and tea. He told her of course, she needn't ask. She stood uncertainly, clutching Louisa's clothing. One of the others passed her. He said he had left the lamp lit for her. It was clear that he expected her to return to clean up the kitchen. Nodding, she hurried out into the snow and ran, almost blindly, to the palace car.

Back inside, she set a last pot of tea to steep on the stove. When Louisa started coughing again, Nell carried a cup of tea up to the berth. Louisa's clammy hand trembled so violently, Nell had to hold the cup for her. After Louisa finished the tea, Nell pulled the covers up tight and tucked her in.

Nell went about the palace car setting chairs and cushions in place and wiping some of the grimier surfaces with a damp rag. At the door she read over the letter to Mr. Hargrove and Mr. Steele.

There was room beneath Joe's signature for a postscript, so she dipped the pen and wrote at the bottom of the sheet: "Louisa has a bad cough. We hurry away to bring her to a doctor." There, she thought, examining the entire message. Now they needn't take offense at Joe leaving like this.

Nell continued dusting for a while, flicking the rag over lamp chimneys and cut-glass sconces, wiping smears from the mirrors. Last of all, she checked the drawer with the books. She picked up *David Copperfield* and settled with it in the elegant throne chair. But there was hardly any light there. She had to start at the beginning because she knew it by heart. "Whether I shall turn out to be the hero of my own life . . ." She dozed off with the book open before her, the dust cloth draped across her knees.

✻ ✻ ✻ ✻ ✻ ✻ ✻ ✻ ✻ ✻ ✻ ✻ ✻ ✻ ✻

29/True Spring

N ell lifted the OPEN sign, ready to turn it, then paused for one last look inside Macomber's Dry Goods Store. Here in front the crockery, the earthen and tin ware; the bolts of cloth, staple and fancy, high up beside the lamps; the wallpaper rolls and trunks set in back under the shelves. Nell knew how much more was crammed from floor to ceiling. She loved the way every single item had its place. After nearly three months she could put her hands on almost anything a customer asked for.

By now she must have seen every person in Pawnook, and they all seemed to know her, too. They would ask how Jessie and the baby were getting on, or remark that only a spell ago it was Jessie who waited on them like this—mind you, not so little a girl as Nell, but able and quick and pleasing.

"Don't forget the insect salve," Peter shouted to her from the road.

Nell had to go back into the new sporting goods department that Mr. Macomber and Peter had all but completed. Mr. Hargrove, who had stopped by one bitter day in late February before returning to Bangor, had advised Mr. Macomber to add a sporting goods section in time for next summer's hunting and fishing trade. Already a freshly painted advertisement on the storefront proclaimed: CAMPING OUT PARTIES FURNISHED—TENTS, GUIDEBOOKS, MAPS, POCKET COMPASSES, AND YANKEE NOTIONS, FISHING TACKLE AND FLY HOOKS AND GUNS FOR THE SPORTSMAN.

But most of these things were still packed or jumbled together. Nell had to clamber over kegs and boxes to find the right tin. She would have been glad for a few more days so that she could help set things to rights, but tomorrow she would be on her way to Upper Medet. Gabe Fowler had written that the roads were dry enough for safe travel; Jessie was eager to go home to him.

Ready at last, Nell turned the sign around to read CLOSED and slipped it over the door handle.

Peter waited for her on the road. She noticed his new haircut first, and then his hands, black with axle grease. Keeping clear of those hands, she asked him whether Mr. Macomber had remembered that they would need more oats for the trip.

"I reminded him," Peter told her. "All he can think of is the wagon. He's still worried about it getting through the mud."

"At least we'll be on proper roads this time," Nell said. "But we mustn't leave without feed for Seesur."

They walked the short distance around the Macomber house to

the backyard. Nell pumped water so Peter wouldn't get grease on the pump handle. He seemed so preoccupied that Nell wondered whether he knew something about the serious talk they were about to have with Jessie Fowler and Mr. and Mrs. Macomber. What if Jessie was going to inform them that she had decided to send Louisa back to the Home?

Right from the start Nell had tried to plead for Louisa. Even that first day when Mrs. Fowler had taken over, bundling Louisa into bed and sending for the doctor, Nell had tried to explain how Louisa needed her. Nell yearned for an end to uncertainty, but no one had time to consider the future. The family was distracted by what had happened with Joe, and then when Mr. Hargrove showed up, attention was diverted once again. It was hard enough nursing Louisa through the fever and cough. Jessie Fowler, who kept the bedside vigil, listened to Louisa's ramblings about Joe and Brother Moose and somehow drew her out of her grieving and back to health. By the time the baby was born, Louisa, who had already opened her needful heart to Jessie, was strong enough to be a willing helper.

It had been a healing time for all of them, Louisa happily engrossed in household duties, especially around the baby, and Peter caught up in the work on the new sporting goods department. So Nell had settled into her own routine in the store, one day slipping into the next, until the snow began to thaw and the swollen river spilled over its low, rocky bank.

Nell could tell when Jessie Fowler started to think about returning to Upper Medet. Some evenings when Jessie was writing to Gabe, Nell saw her pause and gaze at Louisa. It awakened the worry that Nell had almost set aside. Once, she intercepted Jessie's look and almost dared to broach the subject of Louisa's future. But Jessie had smiled, raising her finger to her lips to silence Nell before she could speak, nodding not at Louisa but at the sleeping baby.

Now, at the very last moment, Nell and Peter had been summoned for a talk about their future. Instead of feeling relieved that the waiting was over, Nell had to choke down a kind of seasick sensation that rose from the pit of her stomach.

In the kitchen, Mrs. Macomber nodded them toward the stove. "We've already eaten," she said. "Have yours, then come into the parlor."

Nell ladled mutton-barley soup into two bowls, but she couldn't swallow any. She moved toward the door to the parlor. "They're all in there," she told Peter. "I can hear them."

He blew on the soup. "What are they saying?"

Nell shook her head. "Just voices." She knew that Peter hungered for some word about his grandfather. She could tell when his thoughts were away somewhere north and west of Pawnook. But at least he wasn't brooding anymore. After Gabe Fowler's letter came, informing Jessie that three men, apparently the robbers, had been seen in Woodville, Peter had begun to hope that somehow Joe would find out, too.

Peter sighed. "All right. I'll finish this later." He took one last spoonful before following Nell through to the parlor.

Louisa sat on the footstool near the fire. Baby Adam made snuffly, contented sounds as he lay in Jessie Fowler's lap. Mr. and Mrs. Macomber sat in the big chairs on either side of the hearth. That left the bench. Peter and Nell sat down on it, stiffly, because there was no back.

To Nell's surprise it was Mr. Macomber who spoke. He noted the changes that had come to the household over the past few months, the most important being the arrival of baby Adam, but with other arrivals as well. A house overly full.

"That's a mite roundabout," Mrs. Macomber commented. "Let's get to the matter direct."

Mr. Macomber rose and stood in front of the fire with his elbow on the mantelpiece. He pointed his pipe at Jessie. "Daughter," he declared, "carry on."

Jessie shifted the baby and cleared her throat. She spoke softly, haltingly, about her obligation to the child placed in her care and to the Home that had sent her. The baby began to squirm. Swiveling on the stool, Louisa reached up, and Jessie handed him down to her.

Jessie went on. "It's hard to keep a family going on a small farm when the farmer goes logging all winter. He can miss the best planting time. It's hard and tight."

Nell tried to steal a glance at Peter, but he was sitting so close, she couldn't see him without turning away from Jessie.

"What it comes down to," Jessie said, "is that Gabe and I don't think we can afford two girls and a boy. We need Peter, at least for this coming season." She looked at him. "We hope you'll stay for our sakes. Also for Joe's. He may come looking for you. Gabe thinks he may eventually hear that the man he knifed is still alive. If he does, he's likely to appear, especially if he thinks you're still with us. I surely hope he does. I need to beg his pardon for giving up on him. He never gave up on Nell, nor on me. I need to thank him for bringing you all safe to me, for bringing Adam's cradle . . ."

Peter bowed his head. "I'll stay for now. I'm keeping my grandfather's word."

Nell wondered what Jessie meant to do about Louisa. If the Fowlers couldn't afford two girls, where would Louisa be sent?

"It pleases me that we get along, you and I," Jessie said to Nell. "I was sure we would. It's partly why I wanted a girl, even though Gabe thought we should ask the Home for a boy." She paused a moment before adding, "He certainly never bargained on two girls."

Nell could only nod. Was Jessie Fowler prepared to send both girls away because Nell had inflicted Louisa on her?

"We'd never give Louisa back to the Warburtons," Jessie continued.

Nell, who had been holding her breath, let it out in a long sigh.

"The question was whether to return her to the Home or leave her here."

Leave Louisa with Jessie's parents? Nell glanced at Louisa to see whether she had heard and understood. But the baby had just begun to fuss, and Louisa laid him on the hearth rug, where he kicked and pummeled with his tiny fists. Louisa gave him a finger to hold. Dragging it to his mouth, he sucked noisily. Louisa giggled and called him Mighty One.

"Mighty One?" Mr. Macomber repeated. "What's the child saying?"

Jessie just went on. "Father needs help in the store, especially this summer with the new sporting goods section. Louisa can't help much there."

Baffled, Nell caught her breath again. She seemed to be missing the point. Had Jessie Fowler said something Nell hadn't picked up on?

"But Louisa's good with Adam," Jessie added. "That's where I need help, and in the fields. It doesn't matter so much for her that school is so far. I believe I can teach Louisa what she's able to learn."

Nell was speechless. She swung around to Peter, who was just as taken aback. After a moment he swallowed his astonishment and blurted, "You want Louisa instead of Nell?"

Jessie leaned forward. "That's not exactly—"

Nell found her voice. "You mean to take Louisa for your girl?" But I'm your girl, she wanted to cry. I've been your girl from the start.

Nodding, Jessie held out her hands to Nell, who ignored the gesture. "Sweet Nell," Jessie said to her, "you will do well wherever you are. Louisa . . . Louisa's different. You know what I mean. But we can give her a place, and as she has no name, we can give her ours."

Louisa spoke up then. "Adam will be my new brother."

Nell's thoughts tumbled over each other. Louisa Fowler. She would sleep in the corner room in Nell's bed. Not Nell's bed, never really Nell's bed. Louisa Fowler of Upper Medet, New Brunswick. "What about me?" Nell whispered. But already she knew the answer. She had failed to measure up to Jessie Fowler's expectations.

Just last Sunday, when she had been reading *The Wide, Wide World* and Mrs. Fowler had given her Adam to hold, Nell had been so caught up in the story that a moment later, when Jessie Fowler returned, she had found the baby with his head lolling back from Nell's arm. Jessie Fowler had firmly closed the book and made Nell handle Adam in the proper manner before she was allowed to go on with her reading. Nell hadn't given it another thought until now. How many other failures had there been? Probably hundreds. All the time Nell was worrying about Louisa making a good impression, she had been failing—and failing herself. And now it was too late.

Mrs. Fowler, still leaning, still reaching toward Nell, spoke softly. "It was hard to give you up. *Is* hard. But it isn't exactly giving you up, not if I know you're here with Mother and Father. This is such a good arrangement for you, for everyone. You must see that."

Good arrangement? Nell just stared at her. It took a moment before she realized that Mr. Macomber had reentered the conversation.

"Then," he was saying as he knocked the ash from his pipe, "there's this household to consider. When Jessie and her brothers were growing up, we were used to commotion. But we're older now."

"We considered having Louisa," Mrs. Macomber put in. "Only she does make a good deal more commotion than I want to live with. And Jessie seems to have a knack with her."

"Louisa's doing better already," Jessie declared. "And I know she'll keep improving. Won't you, Louisa?"

"I will. I promise I will." Stumbling to her feet, Louisa faced Nell. "Don't be sad. Say it's all right I was chosen instead of you."

Nell stood up, too. "How long have you known about this?"

"About what?"

"This!" Nell waved her arms. "This plan."

"All day," said Louisa.

Feeling hemmed in by their attention, Nell backed to the window. The chill came right through it, right into her body. Her hands were cold and clammy, her fingers clenched so tight that they seemed locked together. If only she could grasp what was happening. If only she could get beyond the thought that they were leaving her, all of her almost-family, leaving her as her brother had in that time before memory, so that all that remained of him was his leaving her, just that. And then Joe, she thought. How quickly he had vanished that snowy morning when they'd parted on the tracks. But she hadn't been alone then. There had been Louisa and Peter. And now they, too, would be going away.

Gradually Jessie Fowler's voice broke through to her. "We didn't mean to keep it from you. Gabe and I had to decide things. Mother and Father, too."

Nell tried to unclench her hands. She was only a few steps away from the fireplace, but she might have been outdoors. Her fingers felt like ice.

"We'd like you to stay with us," Mr. Macomber was telling her. "And then next fall you can attend school and work for us afternoons."

"We'll do our best for you," Mrs. Macomber added.

Nell could hear them trying to make her feel better, but just now all she could see was the wagon loaded with store-bought goods, the sleigh bobs and the cradle on top. She pictured it trundling away with Jessie and Adam, Peter and Louisa. "And Seesur," she murmured.

"What about Caesar?" Jessie Fowler asked her.

"I'll never see him again." One enormous tear wobbled at the edge of her eye.

"Don't be silly," Mrs. Macomber chided. "This is our family, too. No one's parting forever."

"It's not what she means," Louisa mumbled. "She means it feels . . . feels like Glooskeb going away." She walked across the room to Nell, who made a point of gazing out the window.

"What *is* that child saying?" Mr. Macomber asked again.

Nell looked across the road to the harness maker and on past the barrel factory. She could see people whose names she already knew hurrying through the nippy twilight. The blacksmith's cow, tethered for milking on the other side of the Macombers' house, bellowed for the calf that had been taken from her. Probably the calf was bawling, too, only Nell couldn't hear it. Every night this separation would be repeated until the cow finally submitted, and the calf wandered off to browse on the sweet honeysuckle branching over its fence.

Did a cow remember her calf when it was gone? Did Nell's brother still sometimes wonder about her? There had never been anyone like that for Louisa, no one to have lost, to hope for. Always it had been Louisa who was lost, Louisa adrift among strangers. It was almost as though she lacked the language of family. But not entirely, for she sensed what Nell could not yet put into words, that it felt like Glooskeb going away. It seemed to Nell that each of them must be Glooskeb to the other. Only she had been blind to her own attachment, her need to be needed.

What is that child saying? Most of the time Nell was able to guess. More often than not, Joe had seemed to understand, too. And now Jessie. Louisa wasn't likely to have another tame moose ever again. But if she got one, she wouldn't have to name him Brother.

Nell left the chilly window and returned to the warmth of the fire. There lay Adam, splayed on the hearth rug, defenseless and secure. It was hard to imagine herself ever like that, or Louisa, or even Peter. Could they recover what they had never had, never been? Nell doubted it. But they were not bereft, either, and they were no more alone than the creatures Glooskeb had banished from their common tongue and sent to separate lives.

"Louisa!" Peter groaned. "All this way, and now just Louisa."

"Peter, stop that," Nell ordered.

He broke off, looking slightly shocked that Nell could be so sharp with him at a moment like this.

But in a strange way Nell could feel a part of herself restored. She had spoken to Peter in the old way, and he deserved her reproof.

She wished they had more time, though, time to sort out their feelings and thoughts. Who would Peter talk to about Joe? Even though Peter knew how much Louisa shared his hope that Joe would return to them, it had been with Nell that he had pondered the chances, Nell who could disagree and care all at the same time.

She still had trouble believing that Joe would be changed or reassured. It still seemed to her that people like Mr. Hargrove, who knew what Joe had done, would go on distrusting him as long as he lived, and that Joe would always carry his murderous feelings in his honest heart. But it was the saying and the listening that mattered to Peter and to Nell, the arguments that kept Joe there between them. They would have to find another way now.

"We'll write to each other," she said. "We knew we'd have to do that eventually, when you went off to work on the railroad. We're just going to have to start sooner. And then we'll have more letters to keep."

Starting to shake his head, Peter looked away.

"You can tell me everything," she insisted. "And then, when we meet again, we won't be strangers."

"Of course you won't," Jessie agreed. "Never strangers."

Peter gave a grudging nod.

Louisa said to Nell, "You won't be sad the whole time?"

Nell felt a smile coming on. "Not the whole time," she promised. And then, even though she wasn't reading aloud, her voice caught the lilt of suspense that always quickened at the start of a new chapter. "Listen," she said to them, "we'll be all right. It's just going to take awhile."

Then, for Joe, she added, "You see."

AUTHOR'S NOTE

During the second half of the nineteenth century and the early decades of the twentieth, over 80,000 homeless children were shipped from the British Isles to Canada. Well-meaning programs were established on both sides of the Atlantic, including the United States, to deal with the problem of children who lived on city streets or in work houses, Ragged Schools or shelters, and who were viewed as potential criminals. In New York City alone, the Children's Aid Society sent almost 50,000 children on "orphan trains" to the Midwest, and "boarding out" was adopted by other eastern cities for placing children in rural America.

Some of these children were not orphans. Many of them, separated from siblings and even parents, have left poignant accounts of their lifelong search for their lost families. While some of them found good homes with families they came to think of as their own, countless others were exploited as free labor and abused. Many of them ran away, some remaining rootless all their lives.

Diaries, letters, and reminiscences tell us that for most of these children loneliness was the overwhelming condition of their new lives. Arriving after a wrenching separation and a long journey, a city child was often expected to fit right into an isolated environment that was alien and harsh. Not surprisingly, the country people often viewed these children as suspect because of their city ways. They were thought to bring a criminal element to upstanding rural communities.

The Native Americans of the northeast woodlands experienced a different kind of severing from their past. In the seventeenth century the arrival and settlement of Europeans profoundly affected gradual changes in intertribal territories. Disease alone wiped out more than three quarters of the coastal Native American population. But it was the European fur trade, shipbuilding, timbering, and agriculture in the eighteenth and nineteenth centuries that disrupted their seasonal migrations, destroyed their habitats, and undermined their culture. By the 1870s, when the Micmacs of the Canadian Maritimes and the Passemaquoddy and Penobscot people in Maine had designated tribal centers, territorial confinement was imposed not by tribal separations but by government regulation of their traditional means of livelihood.

Even when forward-thinking writers expressed interest in that vanishing culture (and sometimes romanticized the Indian way of life), a negative stereotype predominated. Thoreau, who went to Maine to experience the wilderness and to learn about Indian lore, was so influenced by that stereotype that he failed to discern the full measure of his Indian guide, a man who became an outstanding leader of his people. Right down to the twentieth century, sensational accounts of Indians stealing white children, often fueled by newspapers like the New York *World,* fired the popular imagination. By the time these stories were proved untrue, they had already reinforced public prejudice against Native Americans.

The less sensational views were simply condescending and distrustful. But there were notable exceptions among white people who lived with and worked alongside Native Americans in towns and lumber camps and on the rivers of the northeast. One of these exceptions was Fannie Hardy Eckstorm, who grew up knowing Penobscot children and their elders, who did business with her father. In the first decades of the twentieth century, when it appeared that little of the Native American culture would survive (except in place names, stories, and vanishing memories), Fannie Hardy Eckstorm devoted herself to its study. Her books on Indian languages and traditions are an invaluable legacy for all Americans.

The growing industry of wilderness tourism, which relied

heavily on Native American expertise, also offered the Indians as part of the colorful woodland scene, much as it lured clients with caribou and moose, by then fast becoming rare in the north woods. Most guidebooks included state fish and game laws. After an unusually heavy accumulation of snow in the winter of 1869, moose almost vanished from the Maine woods. But 1871 through 1872 were light snow years, and by 1873, the moose population began to come back. Guides and operators of sportsmen's camps who were aware of the precarious wildlife balance also knew that the success of their enterprises depended on satisfied customers, and that meant hunting trophies. Every guidebook contained advertisements by taxidermists. In the guidebooks of the period, it is the trappers and the Indians who are most often blamed for the depletion of native wildlife, one 1874 guidebook to northern Maine describing the Indians as "wasteful and improvident by nature."

While timbering and quarrying spurred the branch railways that grew out of the many larger ones that spread through the sparsely populated northeast, it was the tourist industry that upgraded conditions on the trains and made the woodlands accessible to the new sporting trade. Many companies had their own special directors' cars fitted with every kind of luxury. They were used for promotion as well as for recreation. The 1870 Boston Board of Trade Excursion train not only produced a daily paper on its own printing press but also offered its clientele a barbershop, two organs, libraries, and large, well-stocked refrigerators. But the 1870s were also years of frequent rail accidents, and private or corporation directors' cars could indeed end up like Louisa's palace in the middle of nowhere.